ATLANTIS

ATLANTIS

CARLOS BARCELÓ

© EDIMAT BOOKS Ltd. London
is an affiliate of Edimat Libros S.A.
C/ Primavera, 35 Pol. Ind. El Malvar
Arganda del Rey - 28500 (Madrid) Spain
E-mail: edimat@edimat.es

Title: *Atlantis*
Author: *Carlos Barceló*

ISBN: 84-9794-024-5
Legal Deposit: M-48224-2004

PRINTED IN SPAIN

INTRODUCTION

The key lies in Egypt

When we lay people force ourselves to study History and get to the pages about Ancient Egypt we think someone is telling us a tall story or those that worked out the chronology of suffered a mental blackout. It is impossible to explain how this civilisation could have come to be so great, how those empires alongside it pale in comparison, including its successors of Greece and Rome, even though the latter ruled almost the whole world.

It has been scientifically proven that the Egyptians used drills to perform trepanations or to get through great blocks with a perfection that escapes lasers of our times. They also polished metals and some other materials for use as lenses. Their pyramids left a testimony to mathematical perfection for astronomy, at the same time as they invented systems of lighting and ventilation for 'closed' living spaces that nowadays are completely incomprehensible to us... How did they do it?

We are talking about exceptional advances made 4,000 or more years ago by a culture very superior to ours. The fact that in the end they were to be conquered, and physically buried in the desert, does not take away its importance. Above all for our purposes, which are to use them as a reference point to arrive at some very surprising conclusions.

5

The two great theories

Our most important science teachers, the men and women that only find themselves compromised by their own convictions, look for the answer in space. Some even continue to do so now. At the beginning of the sixties, when Asimov, Clark and Bradbury were converting science fiction into a supreme literary quality, while Louis Pauwels and Jacques Bergier were setting in stone their great work *Morning of the Magicians*, we should recognise that they did not have the same information at their disposal as we have today.

For this reason in order to explain the great knowledge we have, for example, of the civilisations of the pyramids, they had to turn to extraterrestrials. Not only was it fashionable, due to the vast amount that was written or filmed about UFO's or 'flying saucers', but there were also no other more plausible explanations.

Imagining the landing of space ships was so inviting that many people saw their occupants teaching the Mayans or the Egyptians how to count using zero, how to cut the great blocks of stone with a precision of tenths of inches, how to use the land and water to obtain the best harvests and, what is more, how to use the latter as hydraulic energy. This may have been true, because the sacred texts of all religions made reference to chariots of fire that lifted into the sky, to gigantic masses of clouds or mysterious beings coming from the mountains or out of strange artefacts, whose images were drawn or shaped, according to how the artists imagined them.

Nevertheless, at the moment that geologists found the best means to extract sediments from the bottom of the sea, while sonar and other electronic methods gave exact measurements of the depths, a surprising reality was discovered: 11,500 years ago the Atlantic Ocean suffered some 'abnormal' geological changes.

These verifications were made by very well-qualified scientists, such as those staffing the Lamont Observatory. The samples that they extracted were subjected to 'Carbon-14' or 'Oxygen-18', which are the most precise systems for 'dating'

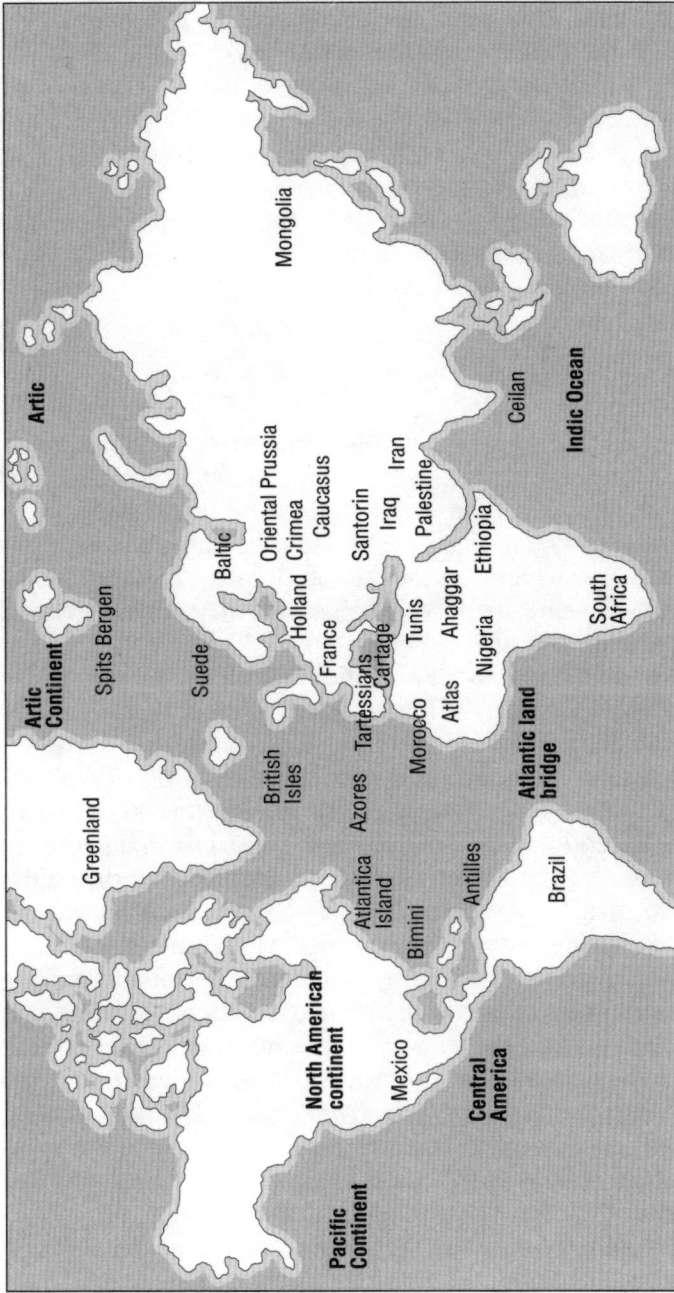

Figure 1. Possible locations where people have have tried to situate the Atlantis mentioned by Plato in his tales.

discoveries. This dates the changes at 11,500 year ago... exactly when Plato said Atlantis had been lost!

We are not going to claim that the second theory was made immediately afterwards; but it did cause the publishing of several not very 'old' books that already proposed it. This inspired new studies, particularly since archaeological excavations showed that in certain parts of the Atlantic, very much related to the existing islands that belong to it now, advanced civilisations had existed earlier.

Nothing is generated spontaneously

Physics tells us that nothing can be generated spontaneously, despite the fact that it may apparently seem that way. Life on our planet was born from some microscopic creatures, with which water, light and other phenomena coincided, all of which together paved the way, in a process of millions of years, for a living being, almost a primate, to stand up and start to walk...

We are talking about evolution, that is to say something long and complicated, that with our present-day mentality we consider logical. Therefore, it is impossible for us to accept the emergence of knowledge revealed in Ancient Egypt. Of course, if we were to suggest the presence of some exceptional beings, to whom some historians refer as 'Red Men', from Atlantis, irrespective of whether they did it before or after the Great Cataclysm that sunk it into the ocean, the suggestion seems justified... doesn't it?

We are going to try to solve enigmas, without worrying about creating others. For it would be absurd to think that we could find all the answers to this mystery. It is important that we follow a historical process, in which we explore the most important paths that lead to Atlantis. For the moment, we will content ourselves with supplying one fact: the pyramid civilisations existed and were so great because of the Atlanteans or the extraordinary 'Red Men'.

Before moving on to the other section, we would like to raise another issue; the world that we are going to discuss is

12,000 years old, approximately, when the first human beings, or something similar, may have existed on Earth for over ten million years. This point becomes a very important one.

The short-sightedness of history

There are many of us that believe that true history is being written by the archaeologists, because as they complete their work across the five continents they unearth 'partial' truths, which they themselves are able to reconstruct within the area that they investigate; nevertheless, they cannot relate it to the rest, that is to say, although they can determine how a tribe behaved, what illnesses they suffered from, the size of its population, what they ate and wore, and other things as well, they cannot ascertain the social and religious pressures, where their predecessors came from or the places selected by their descendants.

The essence of archaeology is to situate certain years, which often reveal no historical answer, because none exists. Nobody would have imagined that dinosaurs had lived in Colorado State (USA) if it had not been for the archaeological excavations that unearthed their skeletons.

In fact, what we know about the past is so little that we should require our governments to work on a reconstruction of History, because that has been manipulated, ever since some 4,500 years ago when the first war took place. Plato was so pessimistic in this respect that he wrote: *at regular intervals, as though it were an inescapable disease, there are cataclysms that leave only ignorant and uncultured peoples as survivors.*

A very clarifying reflection

The Argentine José Alvárez López in his book *Atlantis Reconstructed* offers this reflection:
It is an illusion to think that our scientific history knows something about the human past. The archaeology of the

last one hundred years has taken it upon itself to illustrate how great history's short-sightedness has been. A great number of kingdoms, empires and civilisations appeared, of which there had been no news. It was a true surprise to discover the existence of important Indian civilisations: Mohenjo-Daro and Harappa appeared recently under the spade of the archaeologist, demonstrating that 5,000 years ago there were modern cities, designed by urban experts, with sanitary services at the level of the most advanced urban spaces of current times.

At Mohenjo-Dàro and Harappa they found houses with several bathrooms and running water on the top storeys. The drainage systems, in addition, were works of a modern hydraulic engineering, since they had septic tanks and other technically advanced features. The reality of these discoveries is supported by another recent discovery of the excavations of Thera (Santorini), where the top floor rooms not only had running water, but even hot and cold water. It is important to reiterate Piggot's observation that the modern cities of India lack the comfort they had 5,000 years ago. As the UNESCO publication states, Mohenjo-Daro was a 'Modern City of Antiquity'.

The artistic level of that Indian civilisation, furthermore, was so advanced that we have had to wait 5,000 years for Rodin or Bouerdelle to reach an equal degree of creative evolution. The Harappa torsos mark an apex in the history of universal sculpture.

It was also a surprise to discover the Mochica civilisation in Peru, with great cities, designed for modern urban use, possessing a fully evolved art of portraiture.

All of the above clearly demonstrates how blind we are, as regards the history that we are taught officially... Do we have to find out the truth from archaeology magazines, the great television documentaries and the books written by the most inquiring of authors?

But, to whom do we owe these surprising, unearthed civilisations? Is it possible that great cataclysms have destroyed the physical elements, the spiritual aspects and above all the indispensable memory of their source?

May we go on being surprised

As Egyptian hieroglyphics were being deciphered, happening at the end of the nineteenth century and the start of last century, it could be verified that official history had deprived us of dynasties and kings, like Akhenaton and his El Amarna court, together with the now famous Nefertiti and her son Tutankhamen. This recuperation could be compared to some inept historians forgetting about Julius Caesar and Cleopatra when telling us about what had happened during the Roman Empire.

It is possible that it is so unsavoury to think that there were civilisations more ancient than the Egyptian civilisation which have only been allocated a few pages. For example, in Jericho, close to a spring the most modern city known was unearthed. Someone built it 10,000 years ago, in such a way that modern urban experts would find it impossible to imitate.

Negligence has permitted some civilisations to pass into the 'file of the non-existent' for the simple fact that they were too well mentioned in myths or legends. When these, as has been proved by anthropologists, always have a real origin. One of the most complete examples can be found in the city of Troy, which the German Schliemann discovered in the nineteenth century. Wise historians have declared that Troy only existed in Homer's and other Greek 'fabulists' imagination. The unearthing of this myth should provide rectification and the great Greek author with the title of historian or 'chronicler of his time', in addition to all the other merits that he deserved.

Nevertheless, an excessive number of legends, poems, and millenarian traditions that no-one has managed to place in their historical context remain buried. We do not doubt that one day the task will be accomplished, although we will continue to be ignorant of some of them. Let us recall the passage of Ezequiel in reference to Tharsis:

I shall make thee a desolate city, like the cities that are not inhabited; when I shall bring up the deep upon thee, and great waters shall cover thee; when I shall bring thee down with them that descend into the pit, with the people of old time, and shall set thee in the low parts of the earth, in places desolate of old, with them that go down to the pit, that thou be not inhabited; and I shall set glory in the land of the living; I will make thee a terror, and thou shalt be no more: though thou be sought for, yet shalt thou never be found again.

Religious Studies specialists suppose that the curse was directed at Tartessos, which many consider to be the Spanish-Atlantis. According to Avienus, it was at the mouth of the Guadalquivir. Many archaeologists have looked for it, from Schulten to Arribas, via Maluquer and others, without being able to locate it. There is evidence that Tartessos existed; however, so as to comply with the prophecy, it will never be unearthed.

No myth is superior to that of Atlantis

Above all tales of disappeared civilisations, for its spectacular quality, the one about an island of concentric lakes, situated in the middle of the Atlantic Ocean, described with complete accuracy by Plato in his dialogues *Critias* and Timeaus, stands out.

In the last 2,500 years the force of this island-continent has been so intense, as well as fascinating, that more than twelve thousand books have been written on the subject, while millions of articles and essays, to which we should add, films, comics, and opera and a symphony have been produced. All the scientific capacity of the last two hundred years along with the academic capacity of the last two thousand years has proven too limited in the task of finding the lost civilisation of Atlantis.

According to José Álvarez López: *Geography, Anthropology, Zoology, Botany, Genetics, Mineralogy, Biology, Palaeontology, Archaeology and above all, Geology have all been put into the service of a commendable effort. Thus, throughout one century scientific arguments in favour and against the existence of Atlantis have appeared. The genetic concomitance of the cotton plant has been interpreted by some biologists as a fact that favours the existence of Atlantis. The frustrated migration of birds that still today attempt a descent in the middle of the Atlantic would suggest that there was at some time firm land in those places. The migration of the 'lemming' – the Scandinavian rodent that every 3 and a half years massively migrate toward the Atlantic where thousands of them are found dead – would be explained by the strength of instinct that drives these rodents to swim in the direction of another coast near the beaches of Europe. The migrations of the eel – that lays eggs in the middle of the Sargassos Sea after a biannual excursion through the rivers of Europe – could be another favourable argument to the hypothesis of an ancient firm ground in those places that are today purely maritime. The high level of genetic evolution in some cereals and cultivated plants like the banana plant suggests the prehistoric knowledge of genetics unexplainable without the presence of a great civilisation. The absolute identity of hundreds of vegetable and animal species on both sides of the Atlantic – a surprising fact accepted today by all scientists – proves the existence of prehistoric isthmuses that joined the coasts of both sides of the Atlantic. For certain researchers those bridges of firm land would be very importantly linked to the island-continent of Atlantis. Concluding this interminable list of facts in favour of the existence of an ancient, evolved terrestrial civilisation that has today disappeared, it is appropriate to point out that the advanced technology of certain prehistoric monuments and, especially, the Great Pyramid, is inexplicable in the absence of a civilisation more advanced than ours in the fields of science and technology.*

Geology is our best ally

Until the seventies of last century the most orthodox historians, along with those scientists perversely fond of the 'forbidden', turned their backs on any suggestion of the existence of the island-continent. It was only when Geology proved that transformations occurred in the depths of the Atlantic Ocean 11,500 years ago that people started to take a sideways look at the great enigma.

Today, Plato's dialogue offers a most exciting reality. Through great technological advances – laser, radar, radioactivity, electronics, etc. – it has been possible to revise all of the arguments. Thus the solution to the mystery lies in the ancient Platonic dialogue.

The importance of Atlantis, in conjunction with the mystery that surrounds it, allows us to consider Plato as the pioneer of science-mythology writers. Specialists in science fiction claim that the first science-fiction tale is found in the Egyptian papyrus *Satni Khamoi*, which tells the story of the hero, Neferkeptah's struggle to conquer a book of magic written by Thot, with an army of robots. Later, there was the *Journey to the Moon* by Lucian of Samosata, preceding Jules Verne by some two thousand years.

All commentators add names that we will not include here because Plato's Dialogue is more exciting, it surpasses all the rest. In the same dialogue, Plato describes the island-continent, its landscape, its system of government, its rituals, its geographical situation, the dates of its existence, on top of a great deal of supplementary information such as the solar cycles and the climatic evolution. From a literary point of view, Plato's genius in character setting and the interplay of dialogue to lend veracity to the facts is praiseworthy. There will be few readers that doubt his words.

Where are the enigmas?

The enigmas are as many or more than the paths that we are going to take to explain the different hypotheses related to the locations of Atlantis, as they are with the most important achievements of the Atlanteans. If we begin with the fact that it has still not proven possible to situate the island-continent, we find ourselves faced with the principal enigma.

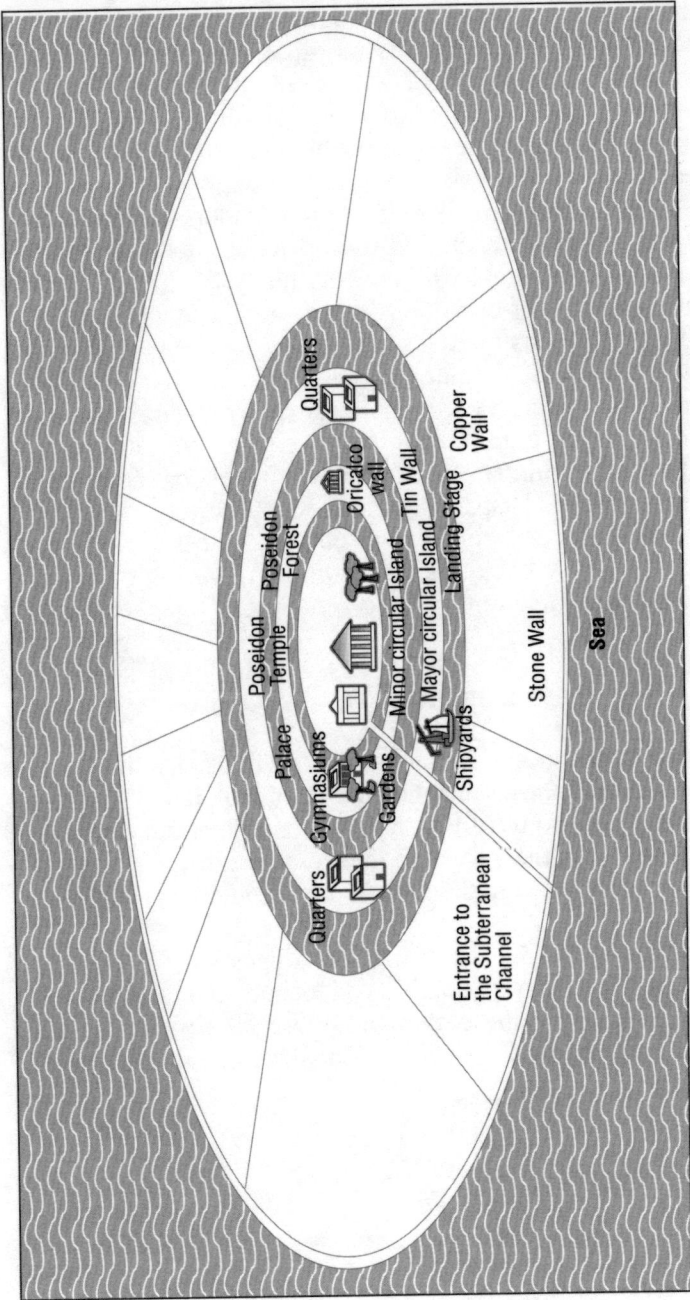

Figure 2. The capital of Atlantis according to Plato's Dialogues.

Quarters

Oricalco wall

Copper Wall

Poseidon Forest

Tin Wall

Poseidon Temple

Minor circular Island

Mayor circular Island

Landing Stage

Palace

Gymnasiums

Gardens

Shipyards

Stone Wall

Sea

Quarters

Entrance to
the Subterranean
Channel

It is best to follow History's signs, because that enables us to learn about incredible, extraordinary events and to deal with fascinating people. The contents of this investigative experience can be likened to a great novel in which the participants seek the same objective but take opposite directions to each other.

All that is left now is to invite our readers to meet a subject that no one can be indifferent to. It would be recommendable to go along with the text, analyse it later, and then investigate further by your own means. Those who live near the Guadalquivir should try to visit the archaeological museums in the areas, consult the old people and local teachers, because they almost certainly know many legends related to Tartessos. We could recommend similar ventures to all Andalusians, Murcians and Spaniards in general, because the influence of this Hispanic-Atlantis was felt everywhere. Juan G. Atienza situates it in the most unlikely places in his forever recommendable book *The Survivors of Atlantis*, a great work of 'field' investigation.

Why indicate so many routes?

All of the routes presented in this book, leading to the localisation of the mythical island-continent, have more to do with the testimony to the imagination of certain heterodox characters than the answer to the Great Enigma. Because that answer is included in the last chapter, along with our reasoning.

Nevertheless, by analysing the suggestions of everyone that has searched for Atlantis', you feel obliged to accept their theories because the explanations are all convincing and, more importantly, they were constructed upon coherent grounds.

Chapter I

AND THUS WAS ATLANTIS

Myth, reality... or a chimera?

If the continent of Atlantis had not existed, someone would have had to invent it, because myths like this one are essential for the human race. An entire world situated somewhere in the ocean, in which one of the most powerful civilisations of antiquity lived, but whose culture was sophisticated to the point of achieving Paradise, lifts the possibilities of creation to the bounds of infinity. However, one unfortunate day the Atlanteans overreached their ambitions, angering the gods. And Zeus, the greatest of them all, fulfilled his role of impartial judge, unleashing a series of cataclysms that annihilated all the inhabitants and then caused the complete disappearance of the island-continent, as it was swallowed by the waves, to leave it in the most inaccessible depths as a testimony to death. It was to never be reborn, having challenged the laws of universal harmony: 'man's greatness must never attempt to overshadow that of the gods.'

The great philosopher Plato, revealing his wisdom in Greece during the fourth century BC, acknowledged the obvious reality of the myth, at the moment when he wrote about it in his dialogues *Timeaus* and *Critias* as something that had existed The facts that he offered were so suggestive, that very few dared to question them. Especially since history came to

17

assist in many men of that time's need to accept chimeras as the best way not to lose hope in human being's limited possibilities.

In such a materialistic world, to affirm that a continent existed, in distant times, whose beauty was one of the most pursued objectives, to the point that they had built mansions and palaces, all surrounded by gardens that the dwellers of Mount Olympus would have envied, stimulated the imagination of the masses. At the same time, it was comforting for them to know that Atlantean sculptors created statues of gold with singular perfection; while, they enjoyed the company of lions, elephants and many other exotic animals that all revelled in absolute freedom. All creatures lived 'together in harmony' in Atlantis.

Moreover, the same story of Atlantis liberated the spirit of the adventurer, making clear that the destruction affected all living creatures and partially the buildings, but not the immense riches... Treasures of incalculable value await the most intrepid adventurers, thanks to gold, silver and many precious stones not being affected by the salinity of the Ocean's water.

The fascination for great mysteries

The majority of religions offer their believers a kind of Paradise, Eden or state of eternal happiness, but they are always based on texts limited by language. The adjectives always fall short when they have to reflect the reward we receive in exchange for an existence under established laws. However, ideas and emotions are easier to stimulate if they are given some specific examples.

Telling the story of Atlantis can fascinate in the great deal of mystery it contains; but, furthermore, it can be linked to Ancient Egypt, where in each of its thousands of pyramids an enormous quantity of mysteries are hidden even today. The subject takes on extra dimensions, now leading to two mysteries. This increases with the more we start to learn: Atlanteans could have been the first Iberians, who made

18

efforts to civilise the inhabitants of the future Iberian Peninsula; and maybe another Atlantean couple began the Basque race as well. In addition, some families managed to escape Atlantis to arrive in the pre-American region of Yucatan, in whose lands they gave rise to the Mayan civilisation.

Having entered the realms of mysteries, we can trace the existence of Atlantis back far before the great continental shift, which would lead us to believe that its inhabitants escaped, having a premonition of the cataclysms that were to destroy the island, in some boats made of papyrus, on which they managed to reach the range of the Andes, settling there to become ancestors of the Incas.

We are not using words as sleights of hand to 'mass-deceive the general public'; all the hypotheses mentioned above are supported by solid archaeological evidence.

A palace that shone brighter than the sun

The palace of Atlantis was constructed under the orders of Atlas, the god Poseidon's son. The marble was extracted from the island's quarries, as were the different-coloured, great stone blocks. The architects designed it according to the Sky and Nature, with the intention of surpassing both, through geometry, understood to be a tool in the service of human genius. Sculptors, painters and other artists all did the same. They took such pains in their creations that the filigrees of just one of the ten thousand columns surpassed the beauty of the most luxuriant of fruit trees or any of the hundreds of birds that populated the gardens.

As every one of the kings occupying the throne of Atlantis took on the task of achieving greater things than their ancestors, the palace was eventually covered, in most part, in sheets of gold, making it shine brighter than the sun. On occasions, around midday, seen from the distance it blinded those that looked upon it, because it was so bright. Moreover, its architecture gave it the most perfect appearance.

In order to prevent any temptation, the palace became surrounded by three great walls, the first made of tin, the second brass, and the third bright copper. In the interior of such a lavish building, several avenues had been laid, provided with a large number of marble, alabaster, and noble wood bridges, which allowed you to cross three moats of constantly fresh water.

The inside of the palace was fitted with the greatest luxuries for the aristocracy: spacious baths, beds made of sandalwood and rooms in which drapes were hung, made with silks of the most exquisite hues. At the same time, the rooms were decorated with evocative marble statues, great vases of flowers and perches for talking birds trained only to speak when spoken to. Plato summarised all this in one sentence:

The wealth possessed by the kings of Atlantis was so immense that equivalent never had nor will be seen elsewhere on Earth.

The Temple of Wisdom

Poseidon's Temple had been built in splendour such as that of the great palace, since it formed the heart of the same. It performed two extremely important functions: gathering the people to celebrate religious ceremonies and as a meeting point for the great leaders to issue laws and impart justice.

It would be said that all the artists who had been involved in the construction of the Temple had set out to emulate the gods, because the decorations, walls covered in sheets of worked gold, the façade coated in silver or the pinnacles of gold, proclaimed the sublime. All those that had the honour to be present inside the immense room, were overwhelmed with emotion when they saw the marble ceilings with gold, silver, and bronze inlays, while the latter also decorated the tall columns and the floor. But all these marvels had been designed in such a way that, upon admiring them, eyes were forced to shift, even involuntarily, to the stunning statue of Poseidon, transformed into the rider of six winged horses, under whose hooves slithered some sea nymphs, offering the attractive image of the most radiant, sensual adolescence.

Another of the Temple's functions was to be the altar for sacrifices. But those were held every five or six years. So the king of Atlantis and his nine brothers arrived there, all governors of the same number of provinces that made up the island-continent. Each one of them was accompanied by the aristocracy and the judges. As the sunrays, entering through a specific point of the vault where a thick crystal had been mounted, met over the centre of the altar, a healthy bull, of some three years of age, placed there, was killed in honour of the gods.

Later, while the animal's corpse was burnt on aromatic woods, the high dignitaries were dressed in black tunics. Some great seats were brought for that moment, and the king, his brothers and the judges sat on them. The moment for new laws to be proclaimed had arrived, and the scribes set to transcribing them onto small gold tablets.

In fact, the continent of Atlantis was governed with great wisdom. Since there was food for all, while the surplus could be traded, it may be said that poverty did not exist. Plato also said, to summarise what happened in that paradise: *Throughout many generations the Atlanteans were cordial, intelligent people, whose nobility of heart enabled them to receive some strangers, whom they treated with generosity...* They had no reason to believe that their luck could change, which is why they persevered with their task of improving themselves. To such an extent that they neared perfection... Is it possible to reach any higher when you have reached the summit of the world? There is always someone crazy enough to try.

The day of the Apocalypse

Atlantis enjoyed a few centuries of paradise, until, in their permanent desire to surpass themselves, they became a continent of warriors. It had never been so. But the 'art' of war can be understood, above all when mercenaries are paid, traitors are bought and the most skilful strategists are teachers. This was how the majority of the Mediterranean countries fell under the control of the Atlanteans.

21

However, war not only releases violence, and since it always goes hand in hand with ambition, the flame of lust was lit in those who had before been moderate in satisfying their appetites. On the other hand, taking up arms discards even the slightest trace of goodness, and they became very cruel. Such were their sins, eventually unbalancing their obsession with owning increasingly more, that the gods became angry. They spent many years sending messages, through the sudden death of some new-born baby in the king's dormitories or the sinking of a fleet of ships. Likewise through the oracles, who, becoming excessively pessimistic, forced Atlanteans to forget their temples.

Then, one bitter day, Zeus himself, the king of all the Olympian gods, called a meeting to decide the fate of Atlantis... Plato decided to interrupt his story at this point; however, it is easy to deduce that the ocean and the earth exploded in the form of a chain of tidal waves and volcanic eruptions. The Apocalypse was taking place, at the end of which the entire magnificent island-continent would be submerged... It disappeared in such a way to survive years later as the myth.

A scientific-archaeological nature

The fact that Plato left his narrative of Atlantis without an end made people believe that he would write the sequel later using Hermocrates; however, there is no evidence of him ever doing so. For José Álvarez López the books *The Republic* and *Laws* should be read as an extension of the history of the mythical continent, due to the fact that both develop ideas about the Perfect State, coinciding with the Atlantean institutions' ideas.

We all know the great influence Plato has had on political ideas and social progress in the last two thousand five hundred years: first in the Greek civilisation; then in the Alexandrine culture; then in the Arab nations; and finally, in the Christian world. He has left his footprints in all, as much in state organisations as in ideologies. There is no doubt that

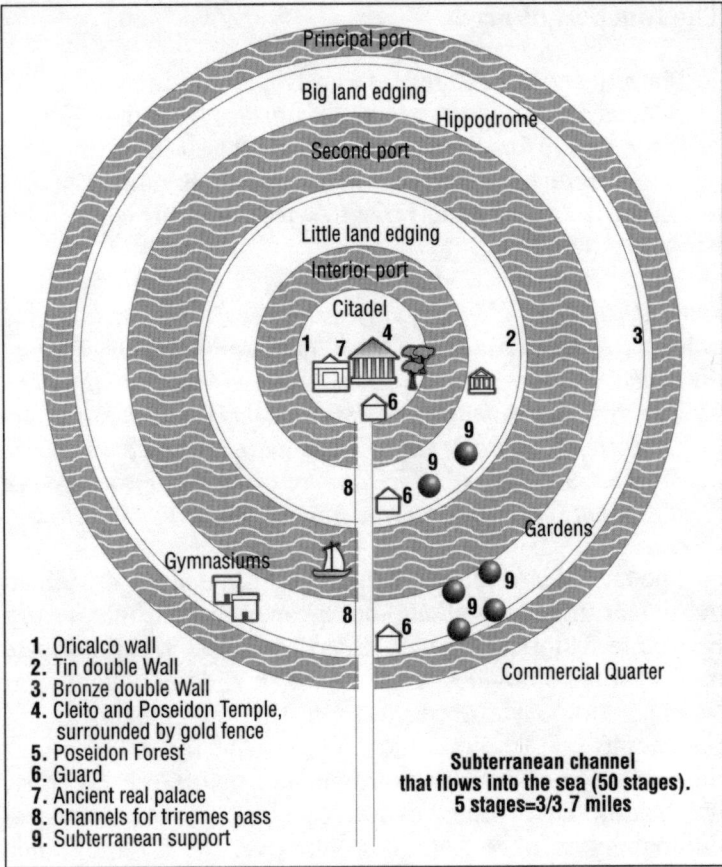

Figure 3. The capital of Atlantis according to Plato's writings.

Plato's tale of Atlantis, besides representing the most important science fiction novel of all time, is one of the main foundations of the civilised world's social and political progress.

It is worth mentioning the cyclical timing of meetings Atlantean rulers followed. They held them every 'eleven years'. The timing Plato presents us with is the same as he used to talk about sunspots, which must mean that the number was decided upon scientifically-astronomically. This proves that Plato was communicating with those initiated in esotericism, to whom he offered some symbols that should be interpreted according to some relatively mysterious keys.

The function of myth

Plato described Atlantis as an island-continent that had existed, which did not stop some historians from thinking it a dialectic tool, using an imagined element to transmit a moral message: unrestrained ambition always leads human beings to tragedy. Philip Young Forsyth wrote the following in his book on Atlantis:

...For Plato the myth fulfilled a very practical function, since it used the element of persuasion. It offered him 'the other way' to arrive at the truth, focussing himself more on the spirit of those that could read or hear his intelligence. That's why the simple truth of the myth was found subordinate to its spiritual content: as Eric Voegelin says, "a myth can never be thought of as 'false', due to the fact that it would not exist without a real base in the movements of the soul it represents".

The fact of considering that all myths are always 'authentic' in spiritual terms should not mean, however, that it must be true in historical terms... Plato had every right to create myths for his dialogues; these myths should be thought of as 'noble fiction', whose poetic truth was fundamental for his philosophy... Plato was more partisan to inventing myths than to using narratives more ancient than Greek society; non-traditional, invented narratives appear double that of traditional myths in the dialogues. Moreover, the few traditional stories that he uses are essentially about the fate of past humanity... We have to recognise that so-called historical myths that made other Greek writers so popular using many real elements are very infrequent in the dialogues. It could be said that this particular kind of myth was not practical for Plato to communicate his philosophy.

What does this stance mean for the myth of Atlantis? First, we have to recognise that it is more likely that Plato invented it than used a true story... That should not imply we have to bury the idea that Atlantis existed. Another circumstance that supports this belief in the 'truth' comes from Socrates and Critias· although, in this case, we should consider it more 'spiritual' than historical. There is no doubt that Plato used myths because they allowed him to represent spiritual truths, and the story of Atlantis certainly suggests an act of divine justice.

On top of all the philosophical conclusions, we have to recognise that Plato created such a solid myth that it inspired thousands of researchers and adventurers to take up the theme again. Thanks to the fact that the Great Enigma invited itself to be resolved, although for that the jungle of facts had to be untangled in such a way that it 'bound' even tighter, leading to some paths that manipulated elements so that in themselves they formed new mysteries. This was the behaviour of some very curious characters, who were shocked by nothing, as we will demonstrate.

The possible location of Atlantis

Plato wrote that Atlantis lay beyond the Towers of Hercules, which, it is thought at those times, meant beyond the Strait of Gibraltar. This locates the lost island-continent in the Atlantic itself.

As for references to the size of Atlantis, Plato indicated that it was greater than Libya (the known part of the north of Africa at that time) and Asia (larger than present-day Turkey). Since it measured, moreover, 3,000 stadiums long and 2,000 wide, bearing in mind that one stadium is equivalent to 610 feet, which results in a measurement of 80,940 square miles. But this only corresponds to part of a continent since Poseidon, the founding god of Atlantis, divided it into ten sections. This leads us to believe, based on an approximate calculation, that the total surface area could be from 625,000 to 740,000 square miles. The mythical island-continent should therefore be slightly smaller than Greenland and over four times larger than the Spanish peninsula. That would be too big to fit within the Mediterranean.

As for the age of Atlantis, in Plato's *Timeaus* a priest tells Solon that it was founded one thousand years before Egypt, which he calculated at 8,000 years old. The sum is easy, and enables us to arrive at approximately 9,000 years old. Since we know that Solon reached the height of his knowledge towards the year 560 BC, we have a definite date, according to Plato's myth, telling us that Atlantis was created in 9560 BC.

All these figures give shape to a reality; however, we will soon come across other historians who place the dates both earlier and later, while the continent moves from location to location according to studies done.

Chapter II

HOMER'S ATLANTIS

The father of Literature

There is no doubt that Homer is the father of universal Literature, thanks to the fact that he wrote in Greek, the language that is considered the best vehicle for creation, and had limitless historical knowledge. Studies have shown that Sophocles was a disciple of Homer, as were other great writers who were students of Sophocles such as Seneca, Shakespeare, Sartre, and Ionesco.

To Homer's merits as the author of works that hold the key to all drama and comedy, and an infinite range of varieties, we must add his position as a prime historian. The legendary city of Troy had always been considered a myth, a city invented as the setting for a literary event, until in the nineteenth century Heinrich Schliemann discovered its ruins. This meant *The Iliad* changed from being a fictional work to a historical document, of unsurpassable literary quality.

In *The Odyssey*, Homer introduces a great number of symbols, which he then uses indiscriminately throughout the narrative. Considered from a scientific perspective, we can reach the conclusion that the name of Homer concealed a group of wise men who wished to leave a message for interpretation with the passing of time.

In regard to *The Iliad*, we have already mentioned the discovery of the ruined city of Troy, but this was due to the fact that Schliemann was able to decipher all the signs left by Homer in order to make one of the greatest archaeological discoveries of all time. In *The Odyssey*, precise symbolism is blended into the wonderful setting to produce an authentic reading pleasure. The work has been esteemed by so many millions of readers that it could be considered the creator of what today we call science fiction. In support of this statement we can remember one of the passages from the epic:

Thence we went on to the island of Aeolia, where lives Aeolus son of Hippotas, dear to the immortal gods. It is an island that floats (as it were) upon the sea, iron bound with a wall that girds it. Now, Aeolus has six daughters and six lusty sons, so he made the sons marry the daughters, and they all live with their dear father and mother, feasting and enjoying every conceivable kind of luxury. All day long, the atmosphere of the house is loaded with the savour of roasting meats till it groans again, yard and all; but by night they sleep on their well-made bedsteads, each with his own wife between the blankets. These were the people among whom we had now come.

Aeolus entertained me for a whole month, asking me questions all the time about Troy, the Argive fleet, and the return of the Achaeans. I told him exactly how everything had happened, and when I said I must go and asked him to further me on my way, he made no sort of difficulty, but set about doing so at once. Moreover, he flayed me a prime ox-hide to hold the ways of the roaring winds, which he shut up in the hide as in a sack – for Jove had made him captain over the winds, and he could stir or still each one of them according to his own pleasure. He put the sack in the ship and bound the mouth so tightly with a silver thread that not even a breath of a side-wind could blow from any quarter. The West wind, which was fair for us, did he alone let blow as it chose; but it all came to nothing, for we were lost through our own folly.

Nine days and nine nights did we sail, and on the tenth day our native land showed on the horizon. We got so close in that we could see the stubble fires burning, and I, being then dead beat, fell into a light sleep, for I had never let the rudder out of my own hands, that we might get home the faster. On this, the men fell to talking among themselves and said I was bringing back gold and silver in the sack that Aeolus had given me. 'Bless my heart,' would one turn to his neighbour, saying, 'how this man gets honoured and makes friends to whatever city or country he may go. See what fine prizes he is taking home from Troy, while we, who have travelled just as far as he has, come back with hands as empty as we set out with – and now Aeolus has given him ever so much more. Quick – let us see what it all is and how much gold and silver there is in the sack he gave him.'

Thus they talked, and evil counsels prevailed. They loosed the sack, whereupon the wind flew howling forth and

Figure 4. One of Ulysses' ships at the mercy of the winds that escaped from the leather bag.

raised a storm that carried us weeping out to sea and away from our own country. Then I awoke and knew not whether to throw myself into the sea or to live on and make the best of it; but I bore it, covered myself up, and lay down in the ship, while the men lamented bitterly as the fierce winds bore our fleet back to the Aeolian island.

Homer's narrative continues with the pardon that Ulysses begs of Aeolus, which does not serve to calm his rage. In consequence of his anger, the Greek sailors end up on the island of the Laestrygonians, where they meet with new and surprising adventures.

The symbols of this brief passage

We must consider the entire chapter of the story in which Aeolus and the winds take part as mythology used by Homer to enrich the story. However, in the events that take place on the arrival of Ulysses at the island of the Laestrygonians, he describes a queen and king as tall as mountains and their subjects as giant people. They all start to throw huge rocks at the ships around the island, to kill the sailors. These people should not be interpreted as creatures of flesh and bone, but rather as erupting volcanoes, constantly spewing incandescent rocks and lava into the boiling sea.

The island of Laestrygonians is a volcanic island, as are the other islands populated by monsters that Ulysses visits on his long voyage, whether occupied by the Cyclops, the worst of which is Polyphemus, left blind in his one eye by the king of Ithaca, or by the goddess Calypso. The idea of this symbolism is backed up by the fact that the first thing sailors see on approaching these islands is a dense column of smoke. Homer also tells us that there were peaceful Cyclops, that is dormant volcanoes, while Polyphemus was erupting and spouted a constant flow of lava in his rage and continued to do so after the sailors had passed from sight. And of course the rocks were thrown in all directions, for which reason Ulysses' ships were able to escape unharmed.

A continuous voyage on the Atlantic

Almost all of *The Odyssey* tells of one voyage on the Atlantic. This was deduced by Strabo, as well as by other classic authors. But within the narrative we can identity two parts: the Telemachus, which tells of Telemachus' voyage around the Mediterranean in search of his father Ulysses; and the adventures of Ulysses himself, all of which take place on the ocean.

It is easy to establish a difference between the two parts, because Telemachus' voyages are short, never longer than two or three days, while the voyages of his father cover far greater distances. Ulysses visits unknown islands inhabited by supernatural characters that seem to be more appropriate to the violent waters of the Atlantic, which the Greeks considered an impossible myth. An example of this is given with the presence of the god Hermes, the messenger sent from Olympus to aid Ulysses. He complains that his mission had obliged him to cross 'so much salt water'. And when the king of Ithaca finds himself on a raft in the waters of the island of Scheria, and he sees the god Poseidon, he exclaims, *"He has come from the lands of the Phaeacians!"* (a tribe that lived in the west of Africa).

Further evidence is given by Homer himself, when he recounts Ulysses' adventures on the island of the Chimacra: *Then we arrived at the limits of the Ocean, where the currents ran deep.*

The winds are revealing evidence

Homer tells us how Ulysses sets his course in favour of the Boreal winds from the North, which is predominant throughout most of the long narrative. These circumstances could not have been possible in the Mediterranean, for any ship that set sail under the Boreal winds would have arrived at any of the southern shores within three or four days. Ulysses also sails towards the African coast under the

Zephyr winds from the West, and the Euro winds occasionally help him to reach the centre of the ocean.

Lastly, the king of Ithaca returns to the Mediterranean when he reaches his homeland under the rowing power of the Phaeacians. It is worth noting that his ships almost always sail in a southeasterly direction, however, when he wishes to return he must do so under oar or with the help of the gods.

Definitive evidence that Ulysses' voyage is mostly on the Atlantic is found in the voice of Calypso, when she tells Ulysses that his only way of return to Ithaca is to navigate with the polar constellation of the Great Bear on the left. Therefore, we are left with no doubt that the Greek sailors had always been sailing west.

According to the study of José Alvárez López, Homer's details are very clear, and owing to frequent references to the winds, we can follow his route, even though it is not openly detailed: the winds, the geography, and the astronomy refer to the Atlantic. The evidence is strong enough to banish any other interpretation.

The importance of the trade winds

The predominant wind in the Atlantic is the trade wind, which always blows in the direction northeast to southeast in the Northern Hemisphere and in the direction southeast to northeast in the Southern Hemisphere. These winds are caused by the thermic currents that originate in the tropical zones of the ocean and that drive stratospheric air toward the poles, which means the air closer to the ground within the tropical climes is pushed from the pole to the equator. However, due to the curve of the Earth, the apparent speed of the wind is reduced, which directs the movement to the west. The combination of the two processes determines the direction of the trade wind, for which reason it always blows from northeast to southeast in the Northern Hemisphere.

On the other hand, the movement of the current is directed toward the pole of the high atmosphere, but descends to surface level on the edge of the temperate zones, causing the counter current trade wind, which in the Northern Hemisphere blows from southeast to northeast. Together, the forces of the trade winds and the counter trade winds determine the movement of great masses of air in a clockwise direction in the Northern Hemisphere and in an anti-clockwise direction in the Southern Hemisphere. It is precisely this circular movement of the Atlantic winds that produces the corresponding movement of the seawater. The ancients understood the atmospheric phenomena in minute detail and described the ocean as a circular current, giving it the name *River Okeanos*. This can be demonstrated in the description that Hesiod gives in *The Shield of Hercules*, as it includes the flow of the 'River Okeanos'. We ought to add that this knowledge was considered by European traders as superstition.

We believe there is no better demonstration of the force of the trade winds on the Atlantic Ocean than the voyage of Christopher Columbus. He set out in a clockwise direction. First he headed south, to travel from Puerta de Palos to the Canary Islands. From there, he headed southeast under the trade winds, by which he reached the Antilles. For the return journey, he headed north via the Azores and, from there, arrived at the Spanish coast under the counter trade wind. His captains, the Pinzon brothers, navigated with more precision, as they had a better knowledge of the Atlantic winds.

A further example of using the trade winds in the Southern Hemisphere is offered by the discovery of the Amazon by Cabral, whose ship was driven there by the trade winds from the Cape of Good Hope.

Trade wind dust

Another fact which ought to be taken into account when we interpret the symbols used by Homer is the trade wind dust, which causes atmospheric darkness in certain tropical zones. Around North Cape and Cape Bojador, in Equatorial Africa, we can see the presence of particles that darken the sky and seem to tint the air red. This phenomenon is caused by thermal currents, which bear dust up from the earth's surface.

It is incredible to think that this process has been going on for thousands of years, and that in prehistoric times it must have caused people great wonder and seemed a divine threat. We believe that this can be interpreted to mean that the land of the Cimmerians, always under a dark cloud due to being in the tropics, was an island or a coast hidden under the darkness of the trade dust.

With regard to the location of the island of the Cimmerians, according to Homer's description, it ought to be nearer to the tropics than is the island of Circe. The reality of the situation can be deduced by what she said to Ulysses: *"You do not need anyone to guide you while you sail your black ship. Raise the mast, lower the sails, and the Boreal will carry your fleet."*

The king of Ithaca continued his voyage south and reached the island of the Cimmerians, where we know that the following took place: *There were the Cimmerian people, in the mist and the clouds, their faces never lit up by the sun's rays, not when it climbed the starry sky, nor when it descended to the Earth, and the malicious night extended its darkness over the mortals...*

This description appears perfectly congruent with the situation in the tropical Atlantic, within a specific area and period. We should remember that the oceans, like everything on our planet, have undergone a series of climatic changes, which means that we cannot base our studies of what happened thousands of years ago on what happens today.

Plato was learned in almost all the disciplines of knowledge, including terrestrial changes. In his work on Atlantis, he demonstrates this. However, what is important here is to underline that Ulysses travelled mostly on the Atlantic, and almost always in the tropical zones.

The volcanic islands

Another demonstration that Ulysses journey takes place in the tropics can be found in the adventure of the island of the Laestrygonians, where the natives have the custom of chewing a plant similar to lotus cane, which is very sweet. Ulysses' companions become addicted to the plant and want to remain on the island forever. Homer calls the plant lotus, but it should be recognised as a different plant. The ancient Greeks were unaware of the existence of sugar cane, though by some strange manner, Homer had learned of it, as he shows by awarding it a different name. It is also possible that in some of these exotic places, there were unusual people who were altering their agriculture after arriving from places similar to Plato's Atlantis.

The islands of the cannibals are also tropical Atlantic islands and could be located in Africa or in the Antilles. And each one boasts its own volcano, as Homer makes very clear in his narration of Ulysses' pass between the 'Scylla' and 'Charybdis', where he comes across the underwater geysers, which must be interpreted as the effect of volcanoes erupting on the seabed.

At last we reach Atlantis!

Plato's description of Atlantis is of a tropical island, similar to those visited by Ulysses. In both, it was possible to reap two annual harvests, mentioned by the phrase *the island was covered in grapes and figs*. This agricultural lushness is typical of a tropical region that has regular rainfall.

None of the animals of Atlantis needed to be kept in stables, even at night. From this we can draw the conclusion that there were no predatory animals, such as wolves, foxes, or lions, and that the climate was warm.

The similarity between Plato's tale of Atlantis and *The Odyssey* is obvious on many other occasions. In the former, the origin of the Atlantean dynasty comes from the carnal relationship between Poseidon and the mortal woman Cleito, while Homer tells us that the dynasty that ruled Scheria was the fruit of the marriage between Poseidon and a mortal woman named Periboea. The shores of the island of Scheria are bordered by cliffs, and the island has a narrow entrance via the mouth of a river, through which boats can

35

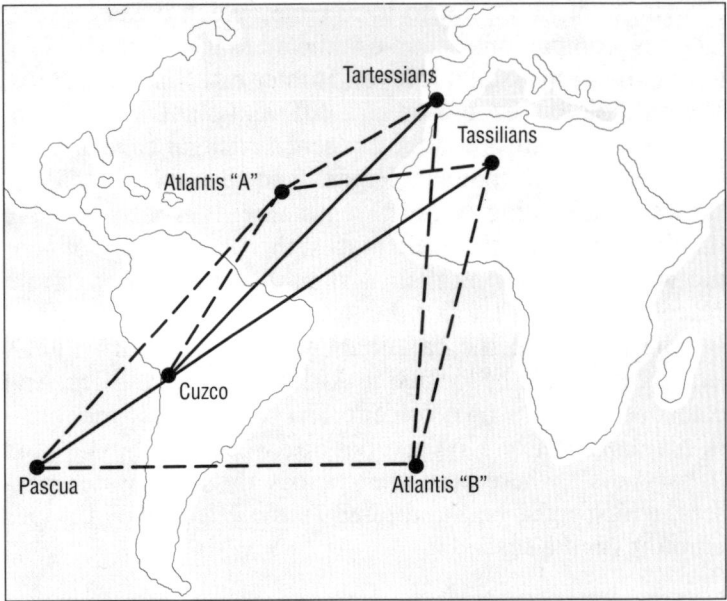

Figure 5. A singular theory concerning the two Atlantis, in which geometric parameters are established between the principal cities of ancient times.

pass. The movement of the tide allows Ulysses to swim through, which also occurs in Atlantis, in which Plato refers to the circular canals that surround the island.

The parallel is more obvious due to the fact that there is a similar situation in the two narratives, in which the boats are housed in covered hangars. The palace of Alcinous, the king of the Phaeacians who inhabit Scheria, is surrounded by constructions with roofs of different metals. All these details make the coincidence between the two texts evident, and as far as the change of name goes, Plato made it clear that the names in his tale had been changed.

Did Homer write science fiction?

In his book *The Reconstruction of Atlantis*, José Álvárez López states the following:

Much has been discussed about the technology of Atlantis provoked by Plato's descriptions of illuminated cites, where immense crowds moved by day and night, and of the gates hung on mountains with covered hangars for the boats, etc. But the Scherian technology – though the Phaeacians lived far from the industrious men – is not left behind. At the end of the eighth verse of The Odyssey, *there is an interesting passage that could be described as 'Science Fiction', which talks of the use of compasses and even of the Phaeacians' automatic pilots. Ancient authors were obliged to use metaphors to describe technical mechanisms, as they lacked the modern terminology to describe such devices. But this cannot raise doubts about what they were trying to describe, as the metaphors are well worded, and the meaning of the language is transparent for anybody who is not opposed to reading what is written. The description of the compass that Homer gives should not surprise us, as we know that the Chinese used compasses thousands of years before Christ. M. D. Coe, of Yale University, has backed up this theory with his studies of Olmec compasses in the form of needles and magnets. The Olmecs were a pre-Columbian race who lived in Mexico during the second millennium BC. They had an advanced culture and a surprising civilisation and had skin of a yellow tint. It is easy to connect Olmec compasses with Chinese compasses; the Olmecs' are surprising for their polished appearance and the precision of the needles, obtained with such a strong yet delicate material as the magnet. We must also remember Homer's relevant text, of which the interpretation must be left open to its readers. Alcinous, king of the Phaeacians, is speaking to Ulysses:*

– Name me also your country, your people, and your city so our ships may fulfil their purpose of taking you there. Among the Phaeacians there are no captains, nor do their ships possess helms like other ships, for they already know the thoughts and desires of the men; they know the cities and the fertile fields of all countries; they cross rapidly the abyss of the sea, through any fog or mist; and they feel no fear of harm or of losing their way.

Figure 6. Bas-relief showing Ulysses and the oarsmen of his ships.

Alcinous is conceding this knowledge to ships provided with surprising mechanical devices, among which could be the compass and a type of automatic pilot, mechanisms that make Ulysses' navigation through the waters of the Atlantic easier, from African coastline to American shores, in a voyage that would allow him to reach Atlantis with ease many times, even though it must have been in the middle of the ocean, 'beyond the Towers of Hercules'.

Chapter III

THE ATLANTEANS IN EGYPT

The Dendera zodiac

Napoleon converted the conquest of Egypt into a military stroll and, above all, into an archaeological expedition of the highest order. Owing to the fact that he was accompanied by great scientists and artists, he forced the world to take a new interest in the great civilisation of the pyramids, after many centuries of intellectual neglect. He knew how to nourish this initial curiosity people with stories of great human, sculptural, literary and graphic richness that succeeded in raising a worldwide interest, which has increased with the passing of time until the present day.

One of the many adventures experienced by the Great Corsican took place in the deserts of Southern Egypt. When General Desaix ordered his army to make a routine stop for rest, a punishing sun drove all men and animals in search of almost non-existent shade. At that moment, there took place one of the events that represent a historic landmark, one of those that marks a huge step in history, but comes about almost by coincidence or by the whim of destiny.

It came about with the simple action of a few soldiers putting a box of ammunition down when the ground gave way under the weight, revealing a black well. On further examination by the surprised soldiers, the light of the sun revealed a stone-walled room, and two men climbed down with torches. By that light, the first of which burned the soldiers' fingers as they stared in amazement at what they were seeing, they were able to see a sight that had been in blackness for more than twenty-five or thirty centuries. One of those discoveries that is so incredible that it almost leaves its discoverers stupefied.

The solders realised they had made a very important discovery and were quick to inform their superiors. General Desaix descended into the room, carrying a better light, and what he saw made him decide to contact Napoleon. This meant various specialists were able to examine the archaeological find, which turned out to be one of the chambers in the fabulous temple of Dendera.

Weeks later, Baron Denon undertook the task of making a series of drawings of the ceiling of the main hall. The task was not

Figure 7. Baron Vivant Denon's reproduction of the Dendera Zodiac, published in 1809 by the Superior Press.

an easy one, due to the lack of light and the positions he had to adopt in order to copy each part. But the finished product was a work of art and can be seen in Figure 8. Napoleon received the drawings when he reached Cairo, and twenty years later, the great stone that bore the Dendera Zodiac was received in the Louvre Museum in Paris.

The evidence of the Great Cataclysm

The ceiling of the great chamber of Dendera drawn by Baron Denon displayed a zodiac 11.81 feet long, 7.87 feet wide, 35.43 inches thick, and weighing 59 tons. As it was impossible to move it in one piece, M. Lelorrain was ordered to cut the stone, which he undertook with great ability, though the hieroglyphic signs referring to the Great Cataclysm were lost: five broken lines representing a great tragedy caused by water, as the appearance of three lines mark the swelling of the Nile and five mean a flood.

At this point, we have to resort to Albert Slosman, an expert in information analysis and collaborator of NASA, who wrote several books about Atlantis. One of them is based on the subject of Dendera, the temple of the Lady of the Sky, where all the foundations of Ancient Egyptian study of astrology and astronomy were found.

This religious building was reconstructed up to six times on the same foundations by the 'sons of Horus', who were thought to be some of the survivors of Atlantis and who arrived many centuries later in Egypt. A papyrus from the time of the Pharaoh Cheops, during whose reign the Great Pyramid was built, proves the temple of Dendera was reconstructed according to the plans left by the sons of Horus on skins preserved in the pharaoh's chambers.

The relation between Dendera and the Great Cataclysm can be found in the word 'pharaoh', which comes from a Greek term that becomes *PHER-AON* or *PER-AHA* when translated into hieroglyphics, which means *he who originates from the firstborn*. The firstborn can only be Osiris – a god related to the Atlanteans who arrived in Egypt, whose name comes from ATH-KA-PTAH, which translated is 'the second heart of Ptah' and pronounced in

41

Greek is *Egyptus*. In this way, they intended to record the Great Cataclysm, so that the following generations would never forget or at least the high leaders, as they were the only ones who could interpret the hieroglyphics and other hermetic texts.

When Atlantis sank

Emilio Bourgon writes in the magazine *Enigmas: I direct the reader to the study carried out by Juan Bonet, an excellent investigator who in his book* When the Earth Turned Over, *published by the University of Navarre, describes the four catastrophes that the Earth has already suffered and points to the possibility of an approaching fifth (turns of approximately 180°), with the consequent cataclysm. All the disasters so far have been associated with different tales of floods in distant legends and traditions, which can be reduced to a maximum of four, and whose characteristics coincide with the four revolutions of the Earth. The last, which coincided with the end of the last glacialisation (that originated the end), was the flood that sank Atlantis told in Gilgamesh's epic and the biblical flood of Noah.*

In this respect, Slosman tells that the priests knew what was going to happen and had built thousands of unsinkable boats called mandjits and not only served to save a proportion of the population, but were also used by their descendants. They are the sacred boats that are recorded in many sources as saving the lives of Osiris, Isis, and Horus.

When the Earth turned 180° on its axis, the apparent movement of the Sun, first it stopped, and later the sky seemed to collapse. Then the Sun doubled back on its course and retreated to where it had appeared, all this in a very brief time. Then there were huge earthquakes and a great flood, and the Sun disappeared.

The survivors escaped in all directions, but many of them headed toward what had been the 'Land of the West Winds', which is exactly what the word *MOGHREB*, the coast of Morocco, means. From there, they embarked upon a lengthy exodus toward the Nile.

The Egyptian drawing as evidence

In Figure 9, we can see the Egyptian sketch that shows the Great Cataclysm that destroyed Atlantis, called *AHA-MEN-PTAH* or 'Paradise lost'. Albert Slosman writes a perfect description of the sketch in *The Survivors of Atlantis*:

The divine triad is found at the head of the fugitives, who had become the survivors of Atlantis, who were to be the origin, with the intervention of Hor (Horus), to a race of Pharaohs or descendants of God.

In the first place is Nut, known as the virgin queen and the mother of Usir (Osiris). She had earned the right to rise to heaven by giving birth to God's first son, and from there she defended the 'inferior brothers'. This led to her being identified with the Milky Way. In the drawing, she appears surrounded by stars, which form a bridge between East and West and is known as 'the great celestial river'.

The enormous continent is submerged in the west, where the horrific tragedy took place. However, only those in the 'mandjits' were able to save themselves, as they were unsinkable boats.

In the boat on the left sails Osiris, wearing a headdress. We can see that the headdress has the hindquarters of a lion, representing the idea of the chaos, destruction, and tragic

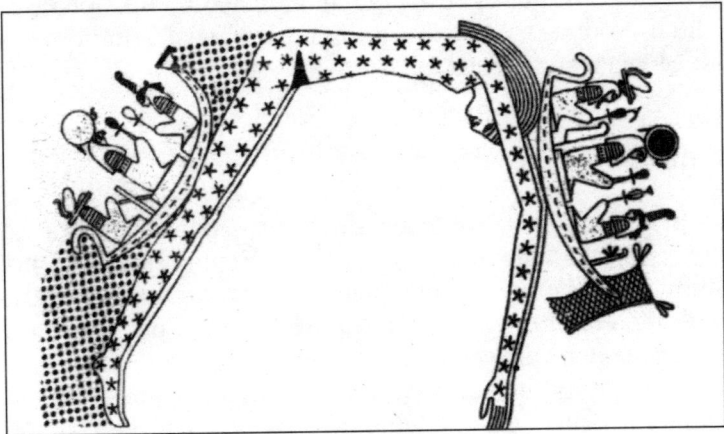

Figure 8. Egyptian drawing of the survivors of Atlantis, aboard the 'mandjit'.

outcome that took place when the Sun retreated through the constellation of Leo. Next to Osiris is his son Horus, under the form of a falcon and bearing the Sun, for its survival depended on the resurgence of the fugitives. He was injured and his life in danger, represented by the bloodstained Ansata Cross, which is not the case with the one that Hor's mother and the wife of Usir, Iset (Isis) bears. She is wearing a green ostrich feather in her hair, which is the symbol of the fugitives from Atlantis.

Lastly, we should interpret that the 'mandjit' on the right has overcome all the obstacles, as it has a 'lucky' sail. Therefore, it was able to reach a point in the East, where TA MANA was to be found, known as 'the place of the sunset'.

Slosman's interpretation of the sketch of the Great Cataclysm allows us to understand many interesting points. One of these has to do with the leap forward that took place in Egypt, which advanced in less than a century from the stone age to the age of bronze or more primary metals. But this surprising evolution did not stop there and led rapidly to an intellectual and creative advance superior to that of any other nation of that area, until it became the precedent for the other countries.

All this must be due to the arrival of the Atlanteans, who brought with them knowledge and created a superior race, which produced pharaohs, priests, architects, astronomers, astrologers, and a great many other creators.

A different approach

In his book *The Challenge of the Atlanteans*, Jean Deruelle discusses the Atlantean influence on Egypt. However, his study starts before the continent had suffered any tragedy, with the cultural influence resulting from the presence of a wise man, who arrived there as a sort of emperor.

The cultural and creative influence that at times reached extraordinary levels was felt during the reign of the Pharaoh Zoser, around the year 2700 BC. We know this from the terraced pyramid of Saqqara, the monumental sculptures, the advances in medicine, the irrigation system, hieroglyphic writing, and the remodelling of moral and religious standards. Deruelle attributes all the merit of this progress to Imhotep, the most well-known intellectual of Atlantis.

It appears that the continent was in danger of losing faith in its deepest principles and made the altruistic gesture of sending one of their most illustrious minds to Egypt. However, Imhotep was not wise only in his intelligence, he was also very prudent. When he arrived in Egypt, he behaved as just another person: he spoke their language, wore the same clothes, had the means to live moderately well, and the colour of his skin was not different enough to attract attention.

For seven years, Imhotep devoted himself to studying the foreign land. He was able to calculate the floods of the Nile according to the movement of the Sun and other stars, and he created the calendar. He also found out where the principal quarries and deposits of the minerals that he would need were located. Once he had all this information, he met with Pharaoh Zoser and presented him with his projects in such a way that the Pharaoh could not refuse them: 'The Great Council of Kings of Atlantis had made the decision to convert Egypt into its heir.'

The best way of achieving this was to transform Egypt into a great empire: The Pharaoh accepted the proposal, and the plans were immediately put into action. But the process would take some time, as groups of cultured people needed to be formed, to transform artisans into artists and constructors into architects of fine buildings. The most simple way to understand is that with Imhotep were other Atlanteans, so competent in the organisation of people that they achieved their target in a very short time.

Thus Egypt became a great civilisation and was to reach sublime heights in almost all areas of knowledge and magic, for the esoteric cult was never left aside. On the contrary, Imhotep manipulated this cult as the ideal vehicle with which to establish fluent communications between the gods and humans via a hermetic religion.

But the question remains: did the Great Council of Kings of Atlantis, knowing that the catastrophic Cataclysm was imminent, want their knowledge to remain in Egypt?

In the History of the world, we know various examples, like that of Moctezuma and his priests, of great empires that knew of their destruction many years before it took place. When permanent contact with the stars is not restricted to the study of celestial movement, but extends to the search for answers for survival, the wise men who achieve these links accumulate such supernatural prowess that, at an unforeseeable point, they are bound to strike a reality that overwhelms them: their own self-destruction. Then they can only hope for the best fate possible. The Aztecs achieved this by fighting bravely, but the Atlanteans preferred to send their intellectuals as transmitters of their great knowledge. Because not only did they reach Egypt, but most advances made in Europe during the Megalith epoch were also due to the Atlanteans.

The Arabs had their idea of myth

Arab tradition also tells of the influence of Atlantis on Egypt, though from a perspective different from those which we have seen so far. In his work *Voyage through the Orient*, Gerar de Nerval writes: *Three hundred years before the Universal Flood, there lived a king called Saurid, son of Salahioc, who dreamed one night that the earth would collapse, people would fall to the ground, and houses would be buried; the stars would collide in the sky, and their fragments would bury the Earth's surface under feet of rubble. The king awoke in fright and ran to the temple of the Sun, where he called all the priests and the holy men. The priest Akliman, who was the wisest among them, confessed that he too had dreamed something very similar...*

From that moment, the king ordered the construction of the pyramids to be angular, so that they would be better able to withstand the shock of the falling stars. And he obtained great blocks of stone, joined with iron stakes and placed with such precision that neither fire, nor water, nor the great flood would be able to penetrate their interior. There the king and the important people of his court would be able to take refuge when the great catastrophe occurred, with books and scientific images, their talismans, and all that would be important in the conservation of the human race...

According to these texts, we must believe that the Pharaohs Cheops, Chephren, and Mykerinus constructed a series of mortuary pyramids, in addition to fulfilling the requirements of being astrological and astronomic observatories, in relation with the threats of the Great Cataclysm that submerged Atlantis forever. Even though there is no mention of intervention by the Atlanteans as instructors of knowledge, it is possible that they intervened in the same way as they were able to provoke these 'nightmares' in the minds of the two most important people in Egypt.

Looting by the Arabs

We all know that the Egyptian pyramids were at the mercy of the Arabs for more than fifteen centuries. Some of the Sultans and Caliphs tried to decipher their mysteries by boring into the stones or looking for secret doors that would enable them to take the treasures out from inside. Many historians blame these actions for the loss of significant documentation, including evidence and details of the relations between Atlantis and Ancient Egypt, as well as the processes of training and instruction received.

We have the Arabs to thank for the recuperation of the talents of Greece and other civilisations, as their Caliphs did not destroy the culture of the peoples they conquered. However, they allowed the pyramids to be buried by millions of tons of desert sand, perhaps because in the looting they did not find the immense treasures they were hoping for.

Gérard de Nerval explains the purpose of the great pyramids: *...The first pyramid was reserved for the princes and their family; the second held the idols related to the stars and the tabernacles of the celestial bodies, as well as the Astrology, History, and Science books, and would also be the refuge* *of the priests. The third was only used to hold the tombs of the kings and the priests...*

Here we have evidence that the pyramids were used as depositaries of the most important information, just like the great libraries of wealthier men, full of knowledge that was written in hieroglyphics and could only be read by intellectuals who understood the language. We cannot say that the Caliphs were ignorant, as most of them surrounded themselves with wise men, but what could have been the case is that, as they did not understand these texts, they did not consider them important, and they were allowed to perish and be forgotten.

The myth is indispensable

In an Arab manuscript translated into French by Pierre Vattier in 1666 and entitled *Le Murtadi*, a scene describes how a group of Arabs found two statues in the *King's Chamber* in the Great Pyramid: one of a white-skinned woman and the other of a black-skinned man. Neither of them appears to have the physical and anatomical features of the Egyptians, and both were found standing on a table. However, what was most noticeable was that one of them was holding a jug carved from reddish glass in both hands, which proved, on examination, to be tightly sealed.

This aroused curiosity about what it contained. Many experts tried to open it, and when one finally succeeded, the jar turned out to be empty. But it weighed too much to be made only of glass, and alchemists were consulted. What happened next is told by the Arab manuscript:

...It was filled with water and weighed again, to prove that it weighed exactly the same as it did empty. In the King's Chamber, they also had found several automatons, and in an adjacent chamber, which resembled a meeting place, there were more statues, amongst which there stood out one of a cock fashioned in red gold. The figure of this fowl was horrifying, in spite of being covered in precious stones, two of which were eyes that shone like lit torches. When they tried to

lift it from the pedestal, it suddenly let out a terrible cry and started to flap its wings, a signal that sparked off a throng of voices that emerged from all around...

Without forgetting the terror that the Arabs who made these discoveries must have felt, we must recognise that the text describes a series of objects and reactions typical of alchemy. The Egyptian priests had known and practised this esoteric science, to the point that they considered themselves its inventors. Can they really bear this merit when we have evidence that attributes the science to the Atlanteans?

In the present day, the mystery of Atlantis not only continues to fascinate all followers of esoteric enigmas, but also maintains the hope that one day we will be able to locate the great vanished island-continent. Many specialists, such as G. Lomer, trust that, one day, a volcanic eruption will produce such a miracle, and all the mysteries will be solved.

Should this never occur, we still have the invitation of Rudolph Steiner, who reverts to metaphysics when he says that *Atlantis will only be recovered through a return of our will to the interior of ourselves*. This must be interpreted as the belief that there are human beings in existence today who can be seen as the reincarnation of an elect group of Atlanteans. According to Léonard Saint-Michetl: *Atlantis is a multi-faceted diamond, which reflects all the images of the world. The myth is always indispensable and capable of nourishing all illusions and faith in the human race...*

But we are at one stage of an exciting journey. After touching on Egypt, we will be very near, and we can advance through the continent following the trail of the great enigma, while we reveal amazing customs and make discoveries comparable to an Aladdin's treasure, providing this was cultural.

Chapter IV

AFRICA, WHERE ANYTHING IS POSSIBLE

In the Sahara Desert

Important historians have situated Atlantis in the north of Africa, where there are various places that resemble the mythical island-continent, amongst which we must underline Mount Atlas. Another element that tempts us to believe this hypothesis is that part of Morocco is indeed 'beyond the Columns of Hercules'.

Part of the most significant evidence has been inherited from the distinguished Herodotus, who lived in the fifth century BC. In the fourth book of his *History* he mentions two peoples that could be related to Atlantis: ...*Ten days' journey from the Garamantes, there is a mound of salt at which water can be found. The place was inhabited by people who are given the name of the dazed, who appear to be, as far as we can decipher, the only beings in the world who have never received a proper name to identify each personally. As a group, they are the dazed, but individually none has a name of his own. These people complain that the sun burns them, and I have heard them insult it with all kinds of abuse. They suffer a great deal from its heat, as does the land where they live.*

After a further ten day's journey, we find another salt mound, also next to a source of water. Here many people live. Quite close, there is a mountain called Atlas. Its shape is narrow and completely round, and it is so tall that its summits cannot be seen from below, as they are permanently swathed in cloud. The local people believe the mountain is one of the columns of the sky, and it has given its name to these people, who are called Atlanteans. And I must say that, according to my information, none of them eat living beings, nor do they suffer dreams or visions...

As we can see, these Atlanteans lack the traits that we admire in the original Atlanteans, unlike those depicted by Plato in his vision of Atlantis. He may possibly have known the works of Herodotus, from which he could only partially take the name.

But Morocco and Mount Atlas are located very near to the Sahara. A very tempting desert, especially when we consider that in the past it was a fertile garden, where rivers ran and there was even an immense lake that was thought by some to be the sea, which was buried under sand and transformed into a mine of petrol and gas for countries such as Algeria and Libya, as well as other riches created by the metamorphosis of the exterior layers of the planet and great masses of water.

The French geographer Berlioux wrote of an Atlantis located in the Sahara Desert, which inspired the writer and poet Pierre Benoit to create an exciting adventure novel of such high quality that it deservedly won every literary prize in France during the 1920s. The book was made into a film in the forties, and admirers of María Montez were able to see her playing the role of *Antinea*, a princess half Cleopatra and half goddess, with a beauty so amazing that she stole the heroes' hearts as soon as they saw her. She ruled over 'the lost world of Atlantis', where the most sublime of the mythical island-continent was represented: the perfection of the decoration, the luxurious clothes and jewels, the paradisiacal gardens, the priestly magic, the strict customs and the charm of unsolved mysteries, which none but a beautiful woman with a mysterious air and Latin blood could have played.

For this reason, it seems profane to recount the events of the novel. It would be much better to read it carefully, as it is written with great literary sensitivity in a style that still seems modern today.

In 1926, Count Byron Khun de Prorok led an archaeological excavation in the Sahara, in the region of Hoggar, where he discovered what is known as the tomb of the queen Tin Hinan (perhaps the *Antinea* that Pierre Benoit had written into his novel years before). The Tuareg believe this queen to be the last sovereign of the Atlanteans, and perhaps for this reason, her tomb was found stacked with precious stones, pieces of gold, beautifully crafted and set jewels, statuettes similar to those excavated in prehistoric sites, and most significant, the skeleton of a young woman, almost adolescent, lying on her side...

Precious discoveries that feed the myth, or revive it, later from unpleasant experiences of the nineteenth century brought about by frauds will be told further on.

The ever legendary Tuareg

The Greek author Pomponius Mela wrote that a fabulous race lived in the Sahara who were known as *blemyes*, because they had no heads. Despite his detailed descriptions and the facts he gives about their customs, several modern historians, such as Henri Lothe, prefer to believe that: *these blemyes were no more than the first wearers of veils, who covered their faces in such a way that, seen from afar, they may have seemed to be headless.*

Those that did have heads were the legendary Tuareg race, called by their desert 'neighbours' the 'blue men', due to their custom of wearing indigo blue robes, which the heat caused to run and tint the skin underneath. As North African legend tells, those born in Atlantis were of blue skin, the famous desert nomads are considered to originate from the mythical island-continent. We have mentioned queen Tin Hinan and her relevance to the Tuareg. This could relate the origins of the desert tribe, who have suffered so greatly at the hands of modern civilisation and are now practically decimated, to Atlantis, and we consider it probable.

The ancient country of Benin

The German archaeologist Leo Frobenius situated Atlantis in Western Africa, in the ancient country of Benin, which was located between Nigeria and Dahomey. Frobenius made so bold as to establish common links between this area and some of the most important civilisations of the Pacific Ocean.

The most interesting point is that there exists a tribe in Nigeria called the *Yorubas* that maintains many of the customs of the ancient civilisation of Benin, or the 'African Atlantis', and which are similar to others observed by Frobenius in the American continent amongst the Indians of Toltec, Mayan, and Aztec origin. There are also some very special features shared by the ceramics of the *Yorubas*, the Etruscans, and other Middle Eastern peoples.

As all hypotheses must be based on solid facts, drawn from archaeological excavations, we know that this archaeologist succeeded in opening the doors to Ife, considered the sacred city of the ancient black kingdom of Benin. Here he excavated a large quantity of objects that were notable for their fine craftsmanship and shapes, many of which were not too old, if we consider that we are describing a civilisation that lived between the sixteenth and seventeenth centuries, destroyed by the massive and continuous sweeps of the slave traders.

The idea that some Atlanteans reached Africa is very possible. Those that managed to escape the Great Cataclysm could have followed the coast of the Atlantic and the Mediterranean, to end up settling in lands that appeared hospitable.

Between the Africans of Nigeria and neighbouring countries, trade is carried on in glass beads called *aggry beads*, which have been found in tombs or fashioned according to ancient originals.

The most remarkable thing is that these beads are very similar to others found buried with Egyptian mummies and in

54

excavations carried out in the Middle East. When we ask the sellers where their glass beads come from, they tell us that they have heard their grandfathers talk of tall men, white-skinned with long dark hair, that had descended from the sky.

The many-talented Georges Barbarin wrote about the experience of a British Major from the colonial period, who *one day contemplated how a black tribe (from British West Africa) were walking to the shore of the sea, led by the chiefs and the witch doctors. They all stopped on the sand and, seeing the arrival of a canoe, started to sing. In the boat, there were two natives painted white, to whom the others made innumerable gestures of submission. Finally, after a short conversation between the chiefs and the new arrivals, the boat men got back in their canoe and pushed out to sea. The Major was very impressed and asked the meaning of the ceremony. He was told that it was a very unusual ritual, to recall the time when, after leaving an island that has now disappeared, white men arrived there bringing justice and noble laws, ended the wars and brought many years of prosperity...*

Can we doubt the power of myths, especially when they are converted into religion? Myths and legends are never false, in the most absolute sense, as they are born from truth or created by the most natural needs of the people.

History was written in Tassili

The French writer and investigator Henri Lothe left the world open mouthed when he published his work *The Sahara: Mysterious Desert*, because nobody had dared to even think that a desert that can reach 70°C in some parts could hide something as marvellous, or even more so, as the caves of Altamira or other caves around found Europe. This is what Lothe wrote:

The paintings are a fact; and there are so many that nobody could consider them a casual or imaginative copy of animals observed in a faraway place. On examination, I arrived at the conclusion that they can only be evidence from the most ancient past, comparable with those in the prehis-

toric caves of France. The hippopotamuses and rhinoceroses painted on the stones of Tassali of the Ajjers are the same as the mammoths and buffalo in the famous caves of Dordogne, many thousands of miles away.

The mistrust that could be created in the ignorance of methods of dating these paintings must be banished after the discovery of such an evident site: prehistoric homes, in which were situated a great number of skeletons, of hippopotamuses, elephants, rhinoceroses, buffaloes, and even fish, alongside a great quantity of stone tools, which prove the ancient existence of human beings in the Sahara and give evidence of long periods of water, in which there grew and lived an extensive and varied range of animals and plants.

Figure 9. In the grottos of Tassili there are these peculiar flying characters that resemble astronauts floating 'free of earth's gravity', next to some objects that remind us of certain jet-propelled vehicles.

In the beginning of the Quaternary, until the start of the Neolithic period, between 6000 and 7000 BC, the great desert was populated by steppe fauna: elephants, rhinoceroses, giraffes, large antelopes, and other animals lived in the great plains, alongside lions, hyenas, and other carnivorous beasts. They are all to be found on the walls at Tassili: the hippopotamus looking for food near the crocodiles, who are surrounded by a great variety of fish.

We know that, at the time of the Roman Caesars, there were elephants in Tunisia, where they were used by the Punic armies of Hannibal. Historians have written that these pachyderms were of a small size, perhaps as a result of deficient nutrition. However, in those times, the Sahara, according to the Roman biographies, was already a desert, which would have placed the elephants in the centre of Africa. We can conclude, therefore, that the animals Hannibal had were animals that were accustomed to lands covered with grass, frequent on the slopes of Atlas...

Today, we know the writings Lothe describes were authentic and have been precisely dated as being 10,000 years old – a time that approaches the existence of Atlantis, whose inhabitants, or survivors, arrived in these lands when they were fertile and lush, to instruct its peoples. Another of the singular facts of Tassili are the figures that are drawn on the walls, which resemble astronauts floating in outer space, with no terrestrial gravity, and others that appear to represent something similar to jet engines.

A more dramatic hypothesis links the drying out of the Sahara with the sinking of the ancient civilisation of Atlantis, which fits in with the theory of the world turning 180°, something that must have caused huge disasters on all the continents, even causing the separation of continent masses that were formerly united.

Returning to the discoveries of Lothe, we must add that most of these paintings were photocopied and faithfully reproduced and are exhibited in the Decorative Art Museum in the Palace of the Louvre. When we admire them, we should bear in mind that 'the ancient history of the Sahara was written at Tassili'.

Chapter V

THE MYSTERIOUS ISLANDS OF THE ATLANTIC

What does the Atlantic conceal?

Geologists and oceanographers who have drawn the map of the depths of the Atlantic were careful to underscore a large plateau stretching from the north to the south. The surfaces on both sides there are flat, something like valleys of different depths, but with a certain similarity between them. One approaches Eastern America, and the other almost reaches the western shores of Europe and Africa.

We all know the sea bed is irregular and has some amazing features. Therefore, it does not seem of particular interest that there are high land masses, some of which form islands, such as the Azores, Madeira, the Canary Islands, Cape Verde, and others.

The Azores and the Canary Islands have always been considered ideal maritime locations, since they seem to provide a perfect first way-station for the long voyage across to the New World. The former lie further from the African continent, while the latter are approximately 530 miles from them. The Canaries are only some 60 miles from the coast of Africa, and the islands of Cape Verde are just off Mauritania and Senegal.

These islands, separated by large distances, present so many similar features that some geologists have taken them as proof of their common origin: Atlantis and the Great Cataclysm, which sunk them into the ocean, so that over the course of centuries, or perhaps during a few decades, various reminders of what had been lost returned to the surface. All these islands are volcanic and have similar terrain, and if we consider their dimensions, it is surprising that they are so mountainous, especially the islands of Tenerife and Palma, which are higher than almost all the mountains of Africa and Europe.

The continental drift of the land masses has been accepted, after being joined for so many millions of years, and we take it as a fact that great geological transformations have been caused by volcanic eruptions, huge earthquakes under the sea, and other cataclysms. One of these could easily be the one that submerged Atlantis, which resulted in these islands and those of the Caribbean and other areas of America breaking away.

Little fanciful paradises

These islands share common elements, such as a warm climate, rich and varied flora, and fertile soil. They each also would have sufficient amounts of fresh water, were it not for the inordinate increase in demand from the explosion of the tourist industry; this does not stop each of them from being a little fanciful paradise.

These shared paradisiacal features are a reminder of the motherland Atlantis, which according to Plato's records and the Egyptian documents was the land of Elysium. On Tenerife, for example, we know that in its mountain soils, we can find all the features of the four seasons and ecosystems that make it a botanical garden, where Nature has concentrated the most lovely and varied plants and landscapes. Over the island towers the majestic summit of its volcano, which, though dormant, never ceases to show the immense heat that boils in its interior and adds the element of risk to the beautiful scenery.

With regard to the climate of the Atlantic Islands, we can refer to Homer's quote about the Canary Islands: *there the air is infinitely pure, and the chills of winter are never felt and are unknown in such benign lands.* Such a privileged situation earned the Canaries the name of the 'Fortunate Isles', which is still used today.

The ocean floor

There are an infinite number of volcanoes on the floor of the Atlantic Ocean, formed in a long chain that runs from Iceland in the north to Cape Verde in the south. At the end of the nineteenth century, a group of geologists extracted a mass of lava from the ocean bed, about 550 miles from the Azores. On petrographic examination, it was revealed to have been formed on the surface, in the open air. A very unusual result, as Professor Termier noted in his report:

Figure 10. Atlantis in a bibliographical document found in London in 1912.

The ground that forms today the bed of the Atlantic, 550 miles north of the Azores, was covered with lava flows at the time when it still remained above the surface of the water. As far as we know, it was sunk to a depth of 9,842.5 feet. Since the rugged outline of the rocky surface has been preserved beneath the water, as shown by the extraction of the sharp edges of the lava flows, atmospheric erosion and the marine currents would have levelled out the ridges and smoothed the whole surface.

This explanation allows us to deduce that the lava could have surfaced from one of the erupting volcanoes at the same time as an underwater earthquake occurred in Atlantis. This tragedy could have created the mountain chain of the Atlantic Ocean and the series of islands and other unique geological phenomena. As we have said, this is a reality that modern science has proved.

It has also been demonstrated that all the submerged volcanoes, and those that are found on the islands of the Atlantic, are founded on the same land base that used to be the primitive continental mass. This evidence supports Plato's theory that the continent was lost to the Atlantic, not far from the Canary Islands. This would explain the survivors reaching different areas of the African coast, Southern Europe, and Eastern America. We attempted to show this theory in a previous chapter when quoting excerpts from Homer, because Ulysses' voyage to the tropical Atlantic leaves the possibility open that Atlantis might have been located amongst these islands.

Geological Atlantis

In his book *Atlantis*, Marius Lleget proposes the following: *The conclusions can now be sketched after the first exposition, and we can outline a possible history of Atlantis, as much from a geographical and geological point of view as from its more emotive human dimension, which inevitably we have taken from the texts of Plato.*

In some ancient period, though we know not when, the Azores, the Madeiras, the Canary Islands, and the Cape Verde islands were united in one continental land mass, or formed an immense archipelago, which would have been Atlantis or a significant part of the geological Atlantis. It is probable that the area formed a block with Mauritania and Portugal, forming a southern coast that stretched out from Cape Verde into the Atlantic, to end in the west at an indeterminate point of the current American continent (probably Venezuela if we go by the writings of the illustrious Professor Requena of Caracas).

Over this vast continental bridge, the differences in climate and, therefore, the varieties of wildlife were considerable, while in the northern zone, more mountainous, a climate similar to that of our Mediterranean regions prevailed. The southern zone, drier and hotter, was in many parts almost desert.

But the apparent stability of Atlantis did not last long. A partial sinking of the side of the Antilles created a significant trench, marking the outline of the Florida peninsula, the archipelago of the Bahamas, and the Greater and Lesser Antilles, a particular distribution that permitted at that time the dissemination of a large number of marine animals, which began to appear along the southern coast of the geological Atlantis.

As the cataclysms continued to shake the Earth, some of which originated in the mountain range of the Andes, the continents began to separate. However, some of the platforms joined to Africa by the area of Mauritania remained. According to the studies of Le Danis, one of the platforms fragmented to form the present Atlantic Islands, where a life very similar to that of its origins developed, though on a cultural level rather less extraordinary.

Islands that appear and disappear

The great cataclysms that have taken place in the Atlantic and are related to the appearance and disappearance of unique islands are reminiscent of Atlantis, despite that fact that this was a disappearance on a much grander scale, and of course this land will never reappear from the depths, at least not as more than small Atlantic islands.

The Azores were struck by an earthquake in 1622, and the capital city Villafranca was destroyed by the huge rifts that appeared in the earth. The movements created a tidal wave more than 65.61 feet tall, which swept up trees, buildings, and hundreds of human lives in its path, and left a bitter memory of Plato's mythical island. In 1692 a similar tragedy shook Port Royal, Jamaica, the principal port of the Caribbean pirates. However, in this case it was believed that the earthquake had been provoked by a divine will as an apocalyptical punishment for these great sinners.

The same could not be believed of the earthquake and tidal wave that caused as much devastation as the West Pacific disasters, which flattened the city of Lisbon in 1775. In just a few minutes, more than 60,000 people and half of the cities buildings perished. The greatest catastrophe came from the huge stone walls, where many people ran to take refuge from the storm, but the great rocks were dragged 590 feet by the waves. It is said that the roar was so loud that not only was it heard in Spain and France, but reached as far as Stockholm.

The Roar of Nature when it becomes enraged, with the force of a thousand Titans, the same as engulfed Atlantis. The same also occurred when an earthquake in the eighteenth century destroyed half the population of Iceland. In 1902, a volcano killed all the inhabitants of Saint Pierre, the capital of the Island of Martinique. And the series of earthquakes that devastated cities like Accra and Agadir produced such effects on the Atlantic bed that, when the resulting damage to the transatlantic cables was investigated, it was discovered that in places the sea bed had risen more than 3,280 feet.

If all this seems difficult to believe, no less so is the proven appearance and disappearance of whole islands, as though they were no more than bath toys. For example, in 1811, the Azores were granted a sister isle. It was visited by specialists, and its volcanic origin was confirmed, like the other islands, and it was given the name of Sambrina. It was charted and mapped, but when the maps were sold and made public, the islands disappeared again. A similar occurrence took place with two islands off the Brazilian coast, close to Fernando de Noronha. As they occupied international waters, several countries tried to take possession of them, but the question of property rights never reached the courts, as the islands sank back into the depths.

Chapter VI

THE BOTTOM OF THE OCEAN

The Mesoatlantic dorsal

There is a part of the Atlantic Ocean floor that runs from Iceland to the Cape of Good Hope and even penetrates into the Pacific which is exceptionally shallow. In oceanic terminology, this is given the name of a 'dorsal', since it can be found in the depths in the form of a mountain range. The strings of peaks that cross the ocean floor are called 'thresholds'.

The Mesoatlantic dorsal physically joins the two poles, extending practically all along the very centre of the ocean at an equal distance from America, Europe, and Africa. At the northern end this dorsal meets another one, with peaks reaching up to a depth of no more than 1,640 feet, which runs across it as though it intended to link Europe to Greenland. The historians of Atlantis consider this dorsal, which thousands of years ago was above water, creating a point of union between America and Europe and explaining the modern similarities in the flora and fauna of the two continents, proof of the existence of Atlantis. At the deepest part of the dorsal, where it approaches Argentina and South Africa, there lies another important dorsal. Despite the lack of geological evidence that in the past these peaks broke the surface and formed a great island-continent like Atlantis, there are many geologists and palaeontologists, amongst whom Bailey Willis is worth mentioning, who consider this a possibility, not least to offer an explanation of the similarities between plants and animals of South America and South Africa. It could even be said that they are mirror images of each other.

Marine sediments

Until 1930, the system used to extract marine sediments was Piggott's corer, with which is was possible to obtain examples up to 10 feet long. However, this method produced so many faults that at times it even made studies impossible. In 1950, a new system was developed by Kullenberg, with a cylindrical piston. It was such a simple system that modern day oceanologists wonder why nobody thought of it sooner.

Thanks to the new system, the study of oceanography underwent a revolution. Kullenberg's invention consists of a cable attached to a piston, which is sunk into the sea alongside the cylinder. When the tip touches the bottom, a mechanism stops the descent of the cable, and the piston comes to a halt, while the cylinder is drawn further down by suction. As in all such marine investigations pressures of up to 500 atmospheres are encountered, the force with which the sediments are sucked into the mouth of the cylinder can be calculated. The added advantage of this machine is that it never goes wrong, as the descent of the cable is stopped by an electronic mechanism that is operated as soon as the tip of the cylinder touches the bottom.

Upon examination of these sediments, sands from all the rivers have been found. For geologists, this is very easy to recognise, as they have already studied the sands of every one of the corresponding riverbeds. The most important is that they can identify the geological ages of the sediments and then examine how the levels of sand, gravel, and lime alternate.

A key element in all such investigations consists of what is called 'foraminifer sands', which are found in two varieties in the ocean, according to whether the waters are warm or cold. The sands are formed with the alternation of sediment layers, and this means that oceanologists can see if the sediments were formed in carboniferous or glacial periods. This type of exploration is easily carried out.

The most precise studies are obtained by measuring the concentration of 'Oxygen 18' in the sediments. After completing the work with the efficient 'Carbon 14', we can see if the Atlantic underwent a increase in temperature some 11,600 years ago. These analyses carried out by the University of Miami and the Lamont Observatory have enabled us to confirm that the age of these sediments coincides with the date Plato gives of the Great Cataclysm that sank Atlantis some 11,500 years ago.

The sands of Atlantis

One of the most complex problems that confronted the geologists was that they found foraminifer shells in the river sands, some of which should not have been in such shallow waters. This led them to two concussions: first, that close to these places were islands or continents, where the sands had formed on beaches and river beds, and second, that the sediments were carried there from thousands of miles away by the deepest underwater currents.

This second conclusion is based on the fact that dips in the sea floor cause the water that carries sediment to sink, according to gravity, in the same way as happens in rivers on the earth's surface. Due to the uneven configuration of the seabed, the deepest underwater currents would have had to ascend somehow to the peaks of the mountains, something that in theory is impossible.

One interesting case is that of the canyons of the Mesoatlantic dorsal, which run parallel alongside it. Some geologists believe they have been created by the underwater currents, but more popular is the belief that they were caused by other phenomena.

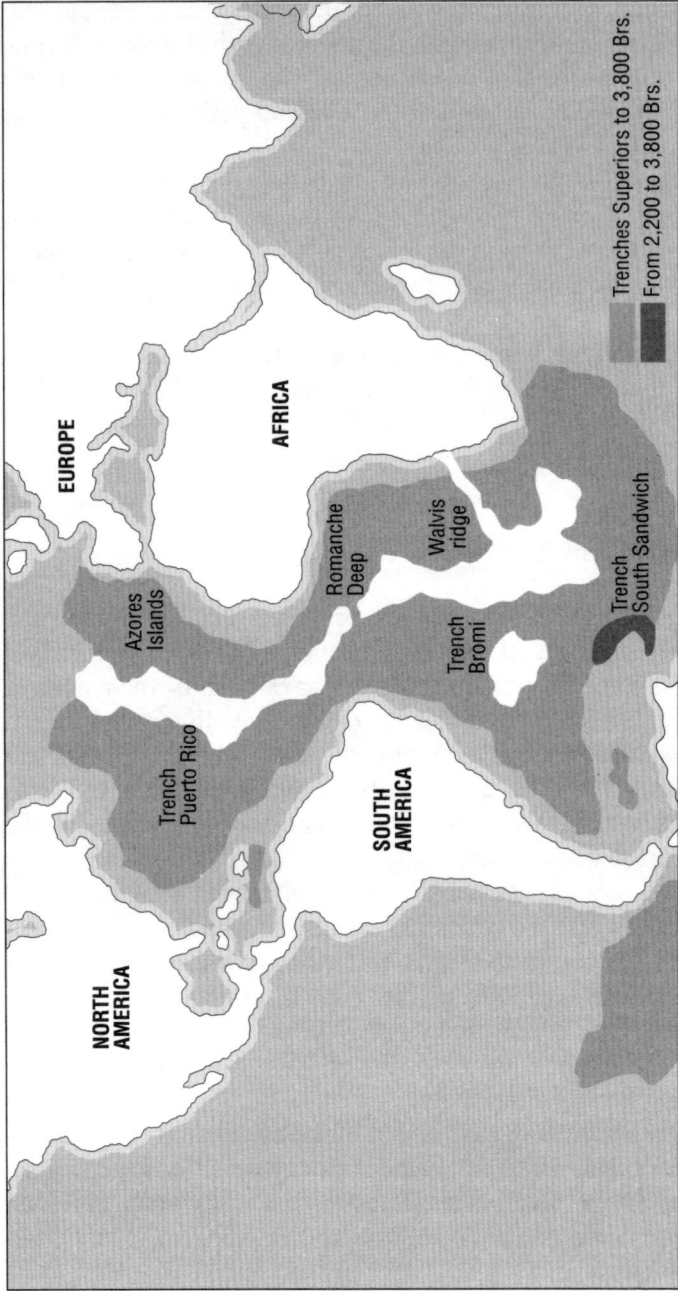

Figure 11. The Mesoatlantic Dorsal.

If we look at Figure 12, we can see that areas where geologists have found sediments made up of sand and foraminifers form a great ring over 600 miles long, which coincides with the possible location of Atlantis. The coasts and rivers of the continent could have formed these sands. However, for the time being this is still no more than a theory.

The Great Cataclysm may have been universal

The geologist K. Turekian carried out investigations in a tropical Atlantic trench, which concluded that 12,000 years ago the content of nickel in the marine sediments decreased by a value of $50 \times 10\text{-}9$ g (cm^2 per year) to $20 \times 10\text{-}9$ (cm^2 per year). This could only be due to the disappearance of a river that used to run close to the area.

It is necessary to bear in mind the figure 12, because this is the date when the quantities of manganese in the sedimentary stratum of the Arctic dropped. It is believed the cause was the invasion of the Atlantic into the Arctic Ocean

In many places on the Earth, Plato's date is given much importance. For example, on the petrified mountain of Wisconsin (USA), it has been proved that 12,000 years ago the fir trees were suddenly buried, and it is a well-known fact that the same period marked the end of the glacialisation of Europe.

A more original opinion is given by the Russian geologist Jaguemeister, as she justifies the end of the glacial period by the arrival of the great current of the Gulf of Mexico, which before then had not been able to reach this zone as it was held back by the immense island continent of Atlantis. When the island sank in the series of cataclysms, the famous Gulf Stream brought warm waters to Europe.

It is also known that the sudden extinction of the mammoths in Siberia took place 12,000 years ago. The famous geologist Cesare Emiliani of the University of Miami, who carried out a series of physico-oceanographic investigations, wrote:

The glacial cap that covered North America suffered a sudden collapse followed by a rapid thaw. Immense quantities of water were carried to the Gulf of Mexico, sparking off a tidal wave that circled the entire planet in 24 hours.

This Great Cataclysm also took place 12,000 years ago, confirming Plato's account: *Atlantis was sunk beneath the waves in a single day and night.*

Geologists calculate that the Earth's sea level rose by some 295 feet at the end of the glacial period. And this would be sufficient to cause the flooding of a string of coral islands such as Atlantis. The most surprising phenomenon is the coincidence of the dates: Plato affirmed the end of the lost continent 9,000 years before his lifetime, which dates the event to 11,500 BC. And the geologists' calculation using the Carbon 14 method that the glacial period came to an end in 11,600 BC supports the existence of the mythical continent.

There is no doubt that the Great Cataclysm affected the whole planet. We have enough proof to demonstrate it and, moreover, date it to a specific time, which also corroborates the existence of Atlantis.

Formation of atolls

Without forgetting the facts of the ocean bed, we are going to investigate some very singular islands, most of which have their origin in underwater volcanic activity. We refer to the atolls. The most popular theory is that these islands came from the existence of the summit of a volcano around which the islands formed, but that then the summit sank beneath the sea entirely.

It is presumed that the thousands of coral reefs that exist in the Pacific are due to the volcanic activity of this ocean bed. For example, geologists believe that during the Cretaceous period, some 100,000 years ago, there were so many active volcanoes on the Earth that they left evidence behind in these coral islands. The reefs consist of a large number of algae, some of which secrete limey substances, including halimeda and lithothamnium.

We all know that the atolls and the reefs are under constant threat from the voracious microbes, worms, and molluscs that bore into them. Many of the romantic atolls seen by Conrad, London, and Gauguin and visited by millions of tourists before the Second World War have now disappeared or are currently on the brink of disappearance, due to the sudden mutation that has taken place in all the coral predators (they have become much more aggressive) as a result of the atomic testing carried out in the Pacific.

Have double atolls ever existed?

We base this question on the fact that Plato's description of Atlantis resembles 'double atolls'. He wrote that the royal palace, the famous Basileus, was built on a triple island formed by three successive circular lakes separated by strips of land. This describes a double atoll, with a huge island in the middle.

However, if our intention is to find out whether atolls existed in the Atlantic in the past, we must remember its volcanic activity. We have already said the geological situations of the past were not necessarily the same as those existing today, so why could there not have been atolls in the Atlantic more than 12,000 years ago?

Enoch's apocryphal book makes several mentions of certain cataclysms that took place in the West:

And the Lord decided to enclose the angels that had shown evil toward men in the valley of fire, in the West, where there were mountains of melted metal, boiling water, a reek of sulphur, and rivers of fire.

Further on in the same passage:

And the sky fell suddenly upon the Earth, and the Earth was swallowed up by a great abyss; and hills crumbled over hills, and mountains over mountains...

Plato did not cite these passages when he wrote of the destruction of the mythical island. He preferred to describe the events in a more sober fashion: *And Atlantis was sunk beneath the waves in a single night and day.*

There are many geologists who do not accept the theory that the Atlantic has had a period of tidal waves, even in the most remote eras. But we cannot forget those that did take place at Thera, Crete, Lisbon, Agadir, and a dozen other places. Even though they were a long time apart, we now have literary evidence that sheds new light on this question.

Hannon's voyage

There is a text about the volcanic activity of the Atlantic that writes of events in the year 530 BC. It tells of the journey of the celebrated Phoenician fleet admiral Hannon, who journeyed around Africa, and contains a valuable description of the ocean at this time, which coincides with all we have written about volcanoes and atolls.

Hannon's intention was to found Carthaginian colonies on the African coast. He managed to establish six, the last of which was at Cape Juby, opposite the Canary Islands. The importance of his expedition was considerable, as the fleet counted sixty ships, each rowed by fifty men, and he was transporting thirty thousand men and women. Hannon passed the latitude of the Canaries and reached equatorial Africa, where his passionate Chronicle describes scenes that are worth mentioning here:

This is the story of the long voyage of Hannon, king of the Carthaginians, beyond the Columns of Hercules. It will remain inscribed forever in stone at the temple of Melkart.

The Carthaginians decided to send Hannon to found colonies. A fleet of sixty ships carried some thirty thousand men and women, provisions, and all the necessary equipment. They lacked nothing, and the spirit with which they sailed assured the success of the journey.

Once past the Columns of Hercules, the first city was founded, which we called Thymiatherion. It dominated an extensive plain.

74

We sailed further on to the west and arrived at Soloei, an African headland covered in trees. There we constructed a temple in honour of Poseidon.

Half a day to the east we entered a lake, a short way from the coast, that was covered with a mass of tall plants, amongst which elephants, bulls, and many wild beasts were drinking and eating.

Some days' sailing beyond the Columns of Hercules, we established five new cities: Karikon-Teichos, Gytte, Akra, Melitta and Arambys.

Continuing our route, we reached the wide River Lixus, which journeys from the centre of Africa, and where the nomadic people take their livestock. We stayed there a while, to acquaint ourselves with the tribe, and formed a firm friendship with them.

In a country ruled by wild beasts and covered with high mountains live a tribe of inhospitable Africans. They tell that the Lixus has its source there and that in the mountains live troglodytes of strange appearance, who according to the Lixites can run faster than horses.

We took Lixite interpreters and sailed south along the coast for two days, seeing nothing but desert. Then we continued a day more to the east. We came across an island no more than a mile in circumference located on the extreme edge of a gulf. There we established a settlement, which we called Cerne. We considered that we were in a position symmetrical with Carthage, calculating that the distance from the Columns of Hercules to Carthage was the same as from there to Cerne.

From that place, we sailed up the enormous River Chretes and entered a lake, on which there are three islands larger than Cerne. We continued our journey for one more day and arrived at that end of the lake, but there was a high mountain there, where savages wearing animal skins threw stones and other hard objects at us. Faced with such aggression, we were forced to abandon the place.

We continued further on until we reached a river full of crocodiles and hippopotamuses, and we decided to return to Cerne.

We sailed south for twelve days, along a coast on which the Africans ran away on seeing us. Their language was incomprehensible, even for our Lixite interpreters. On the last day, we anchored at the skirts of a tall mountain covered with trees, whose wood gave off a delicious scent.

We continued along the coast two days more and found an enormous gulf, where as night fell we could see large bonfires along the shores, dotted amongst smaller ones so that it had an effect of lighting up the whole beach.

We restocked our water supplies and sailed for five days along the coast to an immense bay that our interpreters called 'the Horn of the West'. In the bay was a great island and, on the island, a salt water lake that contained another island. Here we disembarked. During the day, we saw nothing more than the forest, but at night we were able to see fires lit all over the island, and we heard many noises. We panicked and decided to leave the island.

We set sail in all haste and followed a wild coast that gave off a scent of incense. But torrents of fire and lava spewed into the sea, which boiled on contact. The place was very dangerous, and we were fearful of being set alight.

We left the region as quickly as possible and continued sailing for another four days. By night we contemplated a country totally covered in flames. In the centre we could see a flame taller than all the rest, which seemed to reach to the stars. By day it resembled an enormous mountain called the 'Chariot of the Gods'.

At the end of the bay, we found a second island even bigger than the first, again with a lake and a smaller island where savages lived. Most of them were women with stocky, hairy bodies, which our interpreters called gorillas. We tried to pursue them, but we did not manage to trap any of the males, as they kept jumping over the rocks. As they fled, they threw stones at u to cover their retreat, but we caught three females that bit and scratched those who carried them. So we killed and skinned them, to take their skins to Carthage, as our journey was at an end because we had finished our provisions.

76

The significance of Hannon's voyage

Hannon's journey describes what the Atlantic was like in the period before the destruction of Tartessus, or the Spanish Atlantis, told by a first-hand witness. We are left with no doubt as to the existence of large volcanoes and of the geological formations already mentioned.

We should remember, for the sake of fair play, that many geologists have interpreted Hannon's voyage as a journey around present-day Africa, which has resulted in the inability

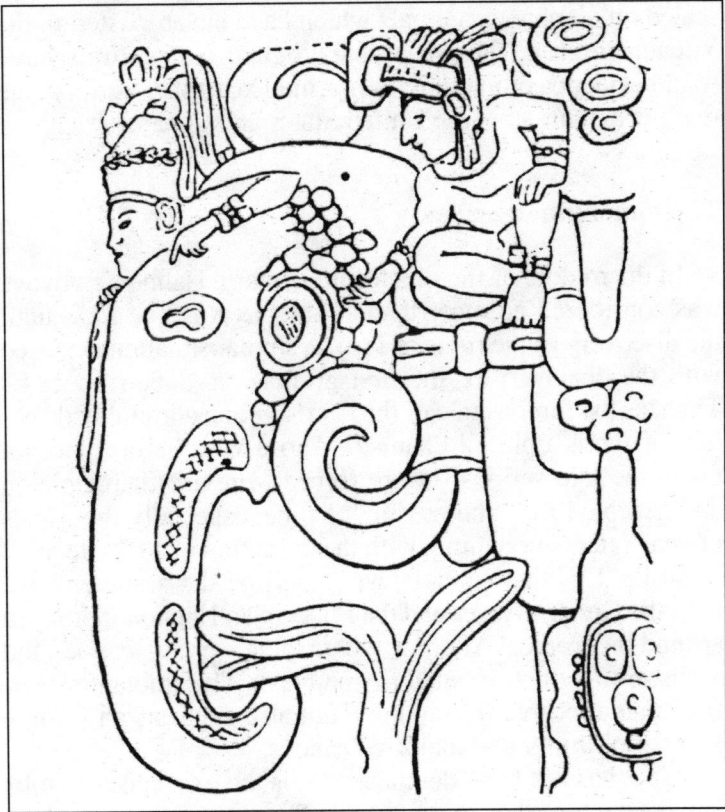

Figure 12. Mayan drawing of priests on the backs of elephants. Could it be a memory of the Phoenicians or the Carthaginians in the region of Yucatan?

to find a single coinciding reference. But this, of course, could be due to the fact that the vast amount of volcanic activity ended up altering the conformation of the islands and the coast, as well as changing the course of the rivers. Today, of that whole scene described covering thousands of miles of fire and flames and rivers of lava that flowed to the coast, there remains nothing more than the small volcano of Cameroon in the Gulf of Guinea.

The other possibility is that Hannon's journey was not along the coasts of Africa at all, but along the coasts of America. That would explain the Mayan drawing of themselves seated on elephants, animals which have never existed in the Yucatan region, though archaeological excavations have found evidence of mammoths in America, further north, in the regions that are now the United States and Canada.

The opportune gorillas

In the middle of the nineteenth century, Hannon's voyage was considered no more than a fable, as was *The Iliad* until the discovery of the ruins of Troy. A similar situation occurred with the discovery of the first gorillas on Gabon, in 1847. Then, as the famous tale of the Carthaginian admiral had spoken of them, opinion changed. Those who before had not taken the tale seriously were forced to revise their opinion and accepted that 'the passing of time, especially thousands of year, alters everything, with the exception of a few details'.

In light of this support, we underline the argument that both the Greek Ulysses and the Phoenician Hannon journeyed around the tropical Atlantic, where there were volcanoes and atolls, from which spouted fire and lava. The amount of bonfires that appeared during the night also suggests an infinite number of minor and major volcanoes.

What has not been demonstrated is the existence of atolls in the Atlantic, when this was what Plato's writings described, with a triple ring. Must we resign ourselves to leaving this question unanswered among the other enigmas? But we can recall the fact that, in many civilisations, the pyramids have been associated with water. In *Popol Vuh*, the Mayan bible, the pyramids are called 'the houses of the fish'.

We are dealing with a passionate subject, which poses questions that cannot be ignored. Is it possible that the first steps of humanity were taken in paradisiacal settings? Is this why the origin of man and woman is set in a *Dan*, an enclosed garden, which in the old Testament is called Eden? Is the westerner's fascination for the southern islands due to the sublimation of a yearned-for paradise? Were the ape-men that Hannon found on an Atlantic atoll simple gorillas or rational, but hairy, human beings?

Chapter VII

ICELAND AND GREENLAND

Hyperborea and Atlantis were the same place

We are not unwilling to admit that we are amongst those who believe that Hyperborea and Atlantis were the same place. D. Duvillé considered that the mythical sunken continent in the Atlantic had been a great peninsula that reached as far as Iceland and permitted direct communication in the north between Europe and America.

The Icelandic alchemist Arne Saknussemm, in the sixteenth century, shared this opinion and believed his country was the last remaining vestige of Atlantis. Moreover, he presented a singular hypothesis: the apocalyptic volcanic phenomena that sank the island-continent caused all the lands involved in the tragedy to be mixed. For this reason, the only place where relics of the disappeared land could be found was the centre of the Earth. And he himself knew the best way to reach the place where these relics could be uncovered.

The first people to foment the myth of Hyperborea were the Greeks, in their nostalgic evocation of what they called the 'Land of the Eternal Sun, where the god Apollo personally went every year, as they were the lands situated beyond the realm of Boreas, who controlled the cold and the storms'.

Once we embark on this new route in search of Atlantis' definite location, we ought to pose another question: do we

81

place the exact knowledge of the Nordic regions in the beginnings of the Middle Ages? We think not. We have sufficient documentation available to tell us that Greek sailors, for example, felt a great desire and curiosity to explore these lands that they saw as loaded with mystery.

Pytheas of Marseilles sailed to territories 'that bordered with the Arctic circle'. The people he found there said to him: 'If you continue rowing another day to the north, you will find the sea becomes solid.' There is no doubt they were referring to the pole. Pytheas had already been surprised that in those remote lands, known by the name of the island of Thule, the nights lasted 24 hours during the summer solstice and days did the same during the winter solstices.

Thule represents another Iceland

During the Middle Ages, the island of Thule was described by the adjectives ultimate, extreme, and misty, but the Greeks were not of the same opinion. They were convinced that the lands were populated by humans with white skin, in some way related to them, for which reason they called them *hyperboreans*. The historian Diodorus assigned them an island as big as Sicily, which he described in the following manner:

Their soil is excellent; its generous fertility provides two harvests each year. As far as I have been able to ascertain, Latona was born there, which explains why the islanders especially worship the god Apollo (the divinity of the Sun). We must consider them almost as the priests of this religion. Every day, they sing songs in his honour and the island bears a great enclosure dedicated to Apollo and a splendid round temple, always filled with numerous offerings. The city is likewise consecrated to Apollo. All the inhabitants play the sitar, which they demonstrate in the many festivals that are celebrated in the temple with hymns and songs of praise. The government of the city and the protection of the temple fall to the kings, called the Boreads, who are directly descended from Boreas, and impart justice with great impartiality...

The Thule described here corresponds to another Iceland, which could never have existed in the glacial period, nor does it resemble modern Iceland. The description above may possibly refer to a time when the island was receiving the benefits of the warm water current from the Gulf of Mexico, in conjunction with a benign temperature that had melted the layers of ice a long time before, revealing a fertile land capable of producing two harvests a year.

However, the populated areas of present-day Iceland can reach temperatures in winter that are above those in Paris, when the average in summer is of 8-10 °C. It continues to benefit from the Gulf Stream that flows around the whole island, as well as from a large number of other sources of warm water.

The Sacred Land

Hesiod situated the paradisiacal land in the north-western Atlantic Ocean. After recounting the annihilation of the race of demi-gods, the Titans, he went on to say:

To others (those who had not succumbed), Zeus, son of Cronus (the Roman Saturn), assigned an existence and an abode and established them on the extremes of the Earth. There they lived, with their hearts free of all sadness, on the Islands of the Fortunate at the edge of the Ocean of deep whirlpools.

He was talking of the 'Holy Land', the Island of *Oggia* or Thule, which has always been identified with Iceland, and in ancient times benefited from a very pleasant climate. It was also known as the 'island of the four masters', which represented the four guardians of the four points of space, the centre of which was the axis symbol, the Pole of the most enriching existence.

Story has it that at the times of the 'flood of Oggia', the 'guardians of tradition' had to take their temple further south, to a place where the longest day (sixteen hours) was double the shortest day (eight hours). And this coincides with the place that is today the location of the solar megalithic temple

Stonehenge, whose stones, according to the Celtic legend, were extracted from the 'island of the four masters' around the year 1700 BC.

Plutarch made use of Silas, in one of his dialogues, to inform us that Iceland is five days' sailing from Great Britain. There the Sun does not disappear for more than an hour or less during a period of thirty days, which means that total darkness is dispelled by a twilight. He then continues with this beautiful description:

The island receives the name of Iceland due to the whiteness of its ice. In earlier times its lands were said to have been fertile, that it had excellent fields and was covered with great forests, which the inhabitants used to build splendid ships.

The Icelandic people are convinced that the mountain Hecla, the main volcano of the island, is the place where condemned souls are tormented, and delightful tales are told about this subject. They say that, on occasion, swarms of demons can be seen entering the caves of the mountain, bearing huge loads of punished souls, and that they soon come out again in search of more souls.

The most fabulous traditions

After the Vikings had established themselves on the island, Iceland and its neighbours continued to be surrounded by the most fabulous traditions. Scandinavian sailors always went to sea in fear of meeting ghost ships, the 'Wafweln', which were propelled by sails made of a permanent flames that unleashed a dreadful whirlwind of sparks as they passed.

The whole of this maritime region seemed to be the setting for many mysterious occurrences related to communication between parallel universes. For this reason, the magnetic storms, so frequent in Iceland, were explained by fantastic and unexpected supernatural manifestations.

The tradition of Thule extends over wider areas than Iceland and even refers to an ancient civilisation whose inhabitants learned to don themselves with fearful magical powers, with which they dominated the cosmic energies and even made contact with intelligent life forms from other worlds.

There is an Indian legend that says: *Some ten thousand years ago, this western land was completely covered with thick forest. Many years before that, pale-skinned men who ruled the thunder and the lightning launched themselves on the wings of the wind to destroy this garden of Nature.*

The Frenchman Bailly wrote in his *History of Astronomy*: *After attentive study of the state of the astronomy in Chaldea, India, and China, we find one that is more related to the remains than with the elements of a science... It is the work of an earlier civilisation. The population was destroyed by a great disaster, which could have been a giant meteorite fall that created a huge flood.*

Figure 13. The monoliths of Stonehenge could have been erected by the Atlanteans.

A Celtic tradition describes the *Sed Jagioug'y Magiouc* (Wall of Gog and Magog): *a monumental wall constructed by a legendary monarch called Skander, who wanted to enclose the Hyperborean nations on the other side of the Caucasus. The wall disappeared long ago, as did the colossal 'boreal column' of Celtic legend, which was said to unite the land with the sky.*

It is also believed that primitive man was white and came from this legendary place called Hyperborea or Atlantis. The Celtic druids affirmed: *Beyond the North Sea there is a land that touches the high walls of Heaven.*

The primitive land of Hyperborea

Esotericism and theosophy have considered that the Hyperboreans and the Atlanteans were the first examples of humanity: their existence goes back some thirty million years, and they are seen as androgynous beings who spent most of their lives in the water. They were gifted with great magical powers and had the spiral as a religious sign. Sergin Huttin writes in his book *Unknown Civilisations*:

These mysterious men lived beyond Boreas, a few thousand years before our era, or even in much later times, as their descendants were known by Greek travellers. They seem to be a highly advanced ancient civilisation that would undoubtedly have left traces in Iceland, Greenland, Scandinavia, Northern Russia, Siberia, and so on (using the modern names of the place beyond the country of the Scythians, as Herodotus said).

Hyperborea seems to have survived the prehistoric glacialisation and the following glacial periods: ancient traditions make it out as an immense terrain located on the other side of the great European quaternary glaciers, traces of which were still visible at the beginning of historical time; on the other side of the icy walls there existed a country inhabited by human beings who boasted dreadful magical powers. According to Chaldean legend, the ancient travellers who arrived in the north, until approximately 4500 BC, were still able to contemplate the great glaciers that shone in the sun, behind which the enigmatic Hyperborean civilisation still stretched, only accessible through a linking tunnel carved into the ice that came out in the Near East near the Euphrates. The great glaciers started to melt more rapidly soon after the fourth millennium and an ocean of mud blocked the way to the land of the Hyperboreans, who fell victim to a formidable flood.

In certain regions, islets of Hyperborea survived throughout ancient times, as was the case of Iceland. But finally, even these traces of the remote civilisation of Thule disappeared: the Irish monks and later the Vikings found Iceland, at the beginning of the Middle Ages, a deserted land.

What happened to the Hyperboreans?

Various hypotheses exist to explain the destiny of the Hyperboreans. One of them refers to the Arian invaders of India who came from the Arctic regions to settle close to the Gobi Desert, in Tibet, Alaska, and even Mexico. The most fantastic of these theories puts the Hyperboreans in the bowels of the Earth, where they perished after living for several centuries without seeing the light of day.

This idea, however, is not shared by H. Bulwer Lytton. In his novel *The race that will exterminate us*, he describes a mysterious realm of human beings who have achieved complete mastery of the forces of magic. They live in extraordinary caverns at the centre of the Earth, which they will abandon in order to become the masters of the Earth. When they come to the earth's surface, they use a cave in Iceland, of which only they know the exact location. The English novelist bases his work on an ancient tradition of Thule, which placed the entrance to the subterranean kingdom in the crater of Snaeffelsjokull, an extinct volcano in the western peninsula of Iceland.

As we can see, the existence of a more important people in other times would not have been so strange. On the contrary, the historian René Quinton attributes a polar origin to the very same and speaks of how the new animals appeared with the arrival of the great cold periods. He writes:

The Poles are focal points of a single origin. All forms given life are no longer susceptible to evolution through remaining captive at the moment of their appearance.

However, we are leaving the subject of Atlantis. We therefore turn to Roger Vercel, who writes of times long before glacialisation. He presents the Hyperborea or Northern Atlantis thus:

Then giant trees made up luxuriant forests in Greenland and Spitzberg. Under a fiery sun, the thick vegetation of the tropics was filled with sap, in the places where we now find lichen growing. The bracken was mixed with huge horsetail plants, with tertiary palm trees and with lianas of the Arctic jungle. There summer shone, and the clouds, brimming with fecundity, let fall a warm rain. And in the immense forest-covered pole lived great animals, the woolly mammoth, the two-horned rhinoceros, the great stag whose antlers measured 13 feet, the lion of the caves. Over the green peaks of the sea swooped birds with huge wings. All this is put clearly in evidence by the coal exposed to the open air in Spitzberg or on Bear Island, this coal where the leaf that turned green, maybe ten million years ago, left a perfect imprint as a testament to a higher past.

In those times, we know that the cold pole lay near Paris or in Eastern Europe, and Earth's paradise extended to the far North of the boreal islands, in the area that is so well guarded by its banks of ice that we cannot be sure where the earth ends and the waters begin...

From this description, we can recognise Atlantis, still in the same ocean, but much further north, beyond the Columns of Hercules mentioned by Plato.

A heavenly Greenland

We know that geological changes can provoke great alterations in the climates, as volcanic activity can change coastlines, deviate rivers, and alter the configuration of mountains and valleys. Many historians explain the huge transformation of Greenland, known a thousand years ago literally as 'the Green Land', with the disappearance of the volcanoes. In Viking times, there were great herds of cattle and lush pastures.

Through the tales of the Scandinavian sagas, we know that the Vikings obtained seals' tusks and skins, as well as butter and cheese from cows. The first product seems logical and the second surprising given the climate and the produce of the island today.

In 1937, important archaeological excavations were carried out in Viking colonies established in Greenland around the year 1000. They inhabited the cities of Eystribyggd and Vestribyggd, where the remains of sheds were found that had sheltered over 300 cows. This was to solve the enigma of the supplies of the three thousand people who lived there in that period.

A wider explanation can be reached through several ancient tales, which coincide in their mentions of a type of geothermic energy. We can read first part of the adventures of the Zeno brothers, taken from the book about the Vikings of Jacques de Mahieu:

The voyage of the Zeno brothers

According to the narration published in Venice, around 1558, by Nicholas Zeno, one of the descendants of the author, of the same name, who sailed in 1380 – later studies show that his departure in 1390 – around the Strait of Gibraltar, with the intention of reaching England. Surprised by a violent storm, they shipwrecked off the coast of Frisland (the current Faeroe Islands). All the crew were saved and welcomed by the king of the island, the Scandinavian Zichni, who spoke to them in Latin to invite them to put themselves into his service. Zeno and his crew, therefore, became integrated in the armada of thirteen ships belonging to the kingdom and helped in the conquest of the neighbouring islands. When Nicholas Zeno was named chief of the fleet, he sent for his brother Anthony, who journeyed to Frisland in safety.

After a series of victorious local conquests, Nicholas set sail in June with three ships. They headed for Greenland, where they visited a convent of the order of Preachers and a church where Saint Thomas was passing the summer, which was built in the crater of a volcano. Near the religious site flowed a river of hot water, which with the construction of underground pipes heated all the nearby areas: the church, the convent, and many gardens, permitting the cultivation of flowers, fruit and vegetables despite the cold polar temperatures. The convent maintained significant commerce with the islands of Norway and Dronthein during the summer months. Ships brought wood, cloths, and domestic animals and carried away skins and, particularly, dried fish, always in abundance due to the vast concentrations of fish that were attracted to the mouth of the hot water river.

The tale of this Venetian coincides with the history narrated by Ivar Barsen, vicar in the fourteenth century in the Greenland bishopric of Gardar. He tells that in these lands there was a lake some seven miles wide, close to the church, where there was plentiful fishing. As the island and its neighbours benefited from several thermal springs, the winters there were warm.

None of this can be found in today's Greenland. The land has changed and little green remains in the desert-like glacial white. Nobody would know that 500 years ago, it was lush and fertile. The geological changes have altered the landscape to such an extent that direct extrapolation to Atlantis has been much complicated. We therefore consider that we should mention the underwater geysers produced in the remote past.

Back to The Odyssey

When Homer describes Ulysses' voyage by the islands of 'Charybdis' and 'Scylla', he tells of a characteristic volcano that is familiar to us. Circe warned the Greeks that if they approached it, half of them would die. But if they changed their course and went via Charybdis, not one of them would survive, as this stretch had a continuous underwater whirlpool that sucked the waters of the sea down and violently spewed them back up. We now can appreciate the reference to the then unknown geological phenomenon: an underwater geyser.

The matter can be demonstrated with clarity if we include Homer's passage, as it provides the best explanation. It is taken from the seventh verse of *The Odyssey*, where Circe speaks:

On the opposite side lie two rocky outcrops. One of these reaches the wide heavens, and its peak is lost in a dark cloud. This never leaves it, so that the top is never clear, not even in summer and early autumn. No man, though he had twenty hands and twenty feet, could get a foothold on it and climb it, for it runs sheer up, as smooth as though it had been polished. In the middle of it, there is a dark cavern, looking west and turned towards Erebus; you must take your ship this way, my intelligent and famous Odysseus. Not even the stoutest archer could send an arrow from this ship into it, because the cave is so high up. Inside it sits Scylla, who howls with more horror than the worst beast.

The second rock is lower, and you will contemplate it, Odysseus, but it is so close to the other that there is not more than a bowshot between them. In this place lies an enormous and violent whirlpool. Three times in the day does Charybdis vomit forth her waters, and three times she sucks them down again; make sure that you are not there when she is sucking, for if you are, Neptune (Poseidon) himself could not save you. On the contrary, you must hug the Scylla side and sail by as fast as you can, for it is better lose six men than your whole crew.

We believe that this paints a very clear picture of an underwater geyser, capable of sinking ships and altering coastlines. If in the case of *The Odyssey* they have the same negative effects as a volcano, then in the case of Greenland, we can see how the Earth's interior heat can be positive when 'tamed' to produce not such a violent reaction.

The similarity between the great legends

If we mention the volcanic activity in the ocean and the nearby coastlines, we can explain the Homeric descriptions

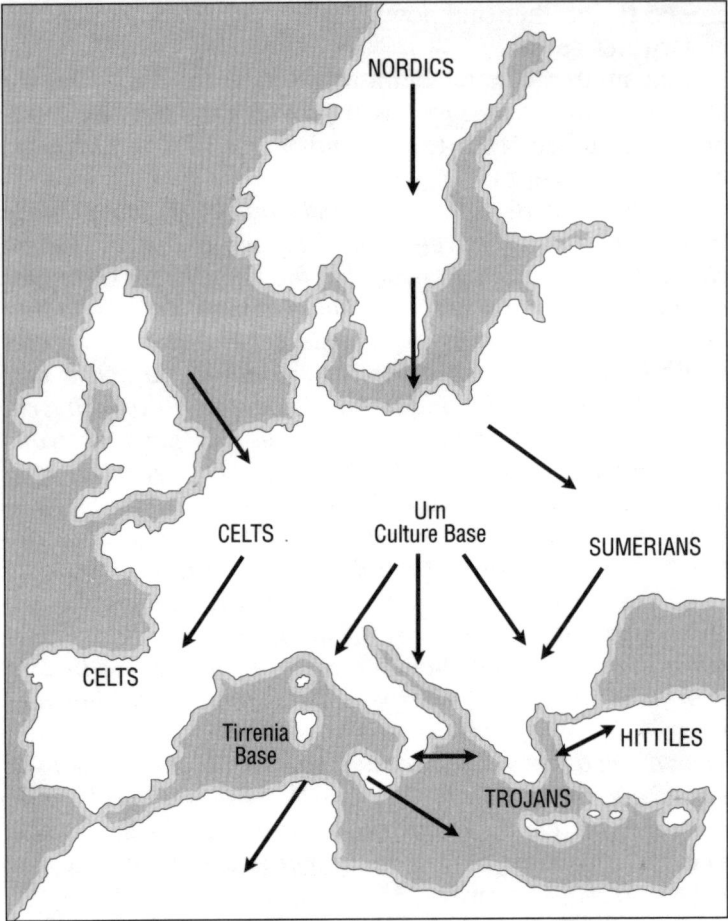

Figure 14. An example of the extensive migratory activity of the so-called 'Peoples of the Sea' in the Mediterranean region and throughout Europe.

of Charybdis and Scylla. This phenomenon does not only affect Europe and Africa, as is logical, but it also reaches the American continent. We could fill thousands of books with the legends of great cataclysms, all collected by anthropologists and travellers, but we must be content with quoting a section from what the Spanish bishop Diego de Landa told the 'Quiche' people of Mexico:

The waters suddenly swelled up and produced a great flood, overcoming all the inhabitants. Nobody escaped the waters, and a dark fog descended from the sky. The surface of the Earth was covered in darkness, and a heavy rain fell. Water poured down from the sky in a torrent during the whole day and night, and a flash of fire passed overhead, lighting up all the desperate men and women, who were running in all directions. They tried climbing on the roofs of the houses, but they were destroyed; they attempted to climb the trees, but they were pulled over; they ran to hide in caves, but they disappeared before their eyes...

As all these legends had a great influence on oral literature, the indigenous ancients took care to preserve them. For this reason, they can be found in the Bible, *The Odyssey*, the Mayan Popol-Vuh, and in many other records. These legends created on all the five continents of the Earth present so many similarities that we are led to believe the tales they relate must be true. What has happened is that they have all undergone slight alterations according to the different culture and the religions of each people.

The considerable parallel between American mythology and the essence of the biblical texts has impressed many scholars and led to hundreds of explorations, in order to explain the information exchange that was created. This, once again, takes us to the existence of the great submerged island-continent as a vehicle of communication between the two sides of the Atlantic.

The Peoples of the Sea

The people that formed the 'Peoples of the Sea' appeared in the Mediterranean around the year 1194 BC. Their origin constitutes one of the greatest enigmas of history. Some historians have demonstrated that they were strongly related to the Etruscan civilisation, while others relate it to Lacedonia, and still others mention Tartessus, whose civilisation we will discuss in the following chapter.

In any case, evidence of this great historical event is to be found in the Egyptian carvings, as Ramses III resisted an invasion from them by executing a manoeuvre to surround them in a battle that is thought to be the first sea battle of all time. However, Egypt was to suffer other invasions, one of which would destroy Syria and the Hittite civilisation.

Wooley did not consider it to be an army, in the exact meaning of the term, as it was made up of by an agglomeration of different peoples. Many of these were entire families, who brought their children and animals with them, although this did not stop them from *destroying Hattusas, which put an end to all reference to the Hittites in Anatolia; they took Carchemis, Aleppo, Ugarit, and Southern Syria. The whole fleet arrived at Cyprus and destroyed it, always advancing to the south, until they came to a halt at the borders of Egypt.*

One of most significant components of the 'Peoples of the Sea' were the Peleset (called Phillistines in the Bible), who later became the Hebrews' worst enemies. It should be noted that the Peleset adorned themselves with plumes of feathers, represented in the Egyptian pyramids, which were similar to those worn by the Toltecs of Yucatan, known as the 'Atlanteans of Tula'. The characters created in the Puerta del Sol of Tiahuanaco also wore similar adornments.

This event may have been a coincidence, but the 'Peoples of the Sea' reached the west after being expelled from the Atlantic islands. Were they forced out by the Great Cataclysm? Today, research still has been unable to clarify the mystery.

Some authors relate the Atlantean invasion described by Plato with the dispersal of the 'Peoples of the Sea'. However, we believe that there was another invasion 11,500 years ago, which was to give rise to the cultures of Jericho, Al-Ubaid, and also Pakistan, because they constitute a representation of some of the lands that, without passing through the Palaeolithic stage, suddenly appeared with a perfectly established civilisation, a developed language, and a social organisation that is surprising to us today. Did they receive all this information from the peoples who had escaped from Atlantis?

There is a possibility that not only the origins of human culture and civilisation come from Atlantis, but that the beginnings of humanity itself were established there. This allows us to associate these beginnings with situations that, in ancient history, encouraged the mental and physical evolution of the entire race, but in the present day is submerged, perhaps due to a great tragedy, beneath the Atlantic waves. We will continue to establish these beliefs as we pass through the events of history, concentrating on those that lead us to different locations that have been attributed to Atlantis.

Chapter VIII

THE SPANISH ATLANTIS

The Tartessus of Andalusia and Murcia

The classical authors cannot agree on the location of Tartessus. Avienus locates it in Cádiz; while Mela, Pliny, Apian, and Stephan of Bizantium place it in Carteia; and Stesicorus, Aristotle, Strabo, and others identify the River Tartessus with the Betis. Modern authors find the same discrepancy in the city's location: Jerez de la Frontera, the island of Saltes, Carmona, Seville, the Huelva River, Coto de Doñana, Cádiz, the mouth of the Guadalquivir River, and so on. Thus the only thing that does remain clear is that it must have been an extensive region, which later was called Turdetania and was somewhere in what are today the regions of Andalusia and Murcia in Southern Spain.

The political organisation seems to have been that the monarchy was descended from the gods, who overcame the mythical kings named by Hesiod in the *Teogonia* (Gestyon, oxen shepherd, Gargoris, the inventor of beekeeping, his son Habis, who taught agriculture and proclaimed the first laws). The only one historically known is Arganthonios, who is said to have lived 120 years and was a great friend of the Phocenses.

Of the religion of the Tartessian people, we know that they had a sanctuary in a cave where they worshipped the *Inferna Dea*; on an island near Cadiz, there was another sanctuary dedicated to the worship of a goddess similar to Venus; and another island in the region of Malaga, opposite Mainake, was consecrated to the Moon. On the coast of the Algarve, there was a sanctuary devoted to the Wind, where sailors worshipped.

The civilisation of Tartessus is a cultural phenomenon of the colonising impact of the peoples of the Eastern Mediterranean, fundamentally the Phoenicians, on the indigenous substratum of the most advanced civilisations of the Bronze Age. This eastern influence, Punic above all, is particularly shown in the craftwork of precious metals (in the treasures of Aliseda and El Carambolo, etc.), the ivory of Carmona and Seville, and the burnished red ceramics pieces that are often difficult to differentiate between Phoenician or Tartessian.

The proximity of the Columns of Hercules

From the first moment that historians began to wonder where Atlantis might have been located, the Columns of Hercules that Plato mentioned always figured very much in their calculations. As the nearest island was Tartessus, many views were focused on that. For example, Otto Jensen wrote that when Plato said Atlantis was bigger than Libya and Asia Minor combined, the place he was referring to was Tartessus, as the great commercial monopoly controlled by the island, owing to its extensive metal exportation to most of the Mediterranean nations; and when he wrote of the 'disappearance in a single night and day', he was actually talking of the conquest of Tartessus.

As we will see further on, this theory has convinced many authors. The fact that Tartessus was an island located further out to sea than Gibraltar, together with its mineral sources and the enormous plain that separated the city from the mountains, encourages the belief that the location for the myth is perfect.

Tartesuss seen as a Cretan or Phocensian colony, born from Atlantis, has been studied by authors such as J. V. Luce, C. Renfrew, and Spiridon Marinatos. However, Adolf Schulten ventured to present the ancient island as a sleeping beauty awaiting the investigator or adventurer who succeeded awakening her from her millennial sleep.

Schulten sees Tartessus as the silver city, the port of the Phoenician and Greek traders, which became so big, it seems impossible it could ever have been forgotten by later generations. An offence that deserved, at least, the amends of the book 'Tartessus: Contribution to the Ancient History of the West', which Schulten wrote:

The name of Tartessus is little known. The Bible frequently mentions Tarsis, especially in the books of the Prophets, which based its riches on silver, tin, and other metals and talks of the voyages of the Tyrians to the west in search of these treasures. There is no doubt that Tarsis and Tartessus are the same city. The indigenous name of Tarsis has been conserved in the River Tertis, as the Guadalquivir was known, at the source of which the city was built. Tertis, converted into Tartessus by the Greeks, was called Tarschisch by the Tyrians, according to a phonetic rule of the Semites, which converts the t *in foreign words to* sch *(Batanbia = Baschan).*

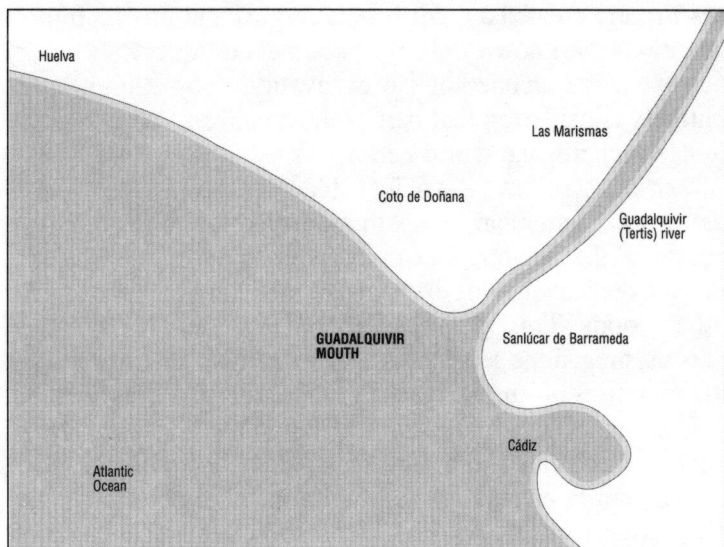

Figure 15. The possible location of the mysterious Tartessus at the mouth of the Guadalquivir.

The oldest contemporary reference to Tartessus comes from the year 730 BC, made by the prophet Isaiah (II, 12-16): "Because the day of the armies of Jehovah will arrive sober and arrogant... and above the cedars of the Lebanon, tall and sublime..., and above all the ships of Tarsis and their valuable treasures." From approximately the same age comes another Assyrian reference, a cuneiform inscription for the king Assarhaddon (680-669 BC), who says: "The kings of the centre of the sea, all, from the land of Jodnan (Cyprus) and the land of Jaman (Javan) to the land of Tarsis inclined themselves toward my plants." Here, as in the Bible, Tartis appears geographically linked to Cyprus and Javan (the land of the Ionians, the Greeks), as a city in the extreme west. The Assyrians, of course, only knew of Tartessus from the tales of Tyrian sailors...

An important metal culture

It appears that during the third millennium BC, the Tartessus Empire created a unique metallurgical culture. Its importance will be known only when somebody decides to carry out extensive archaeological excavations, something that is unlikely considering that part of the area forms part of a designated 'ecological world heritage' site.

Luckily, we have sufficient documentation to know that there were Tartessian routes that covered the most important coasts of the Atlantic Ocean, as well as all of the Mediterranean, dedicated to the exchange of metallurgical products for other goods. This meant that copper daggers, bell-shaped glasses, megalithic sepulchres, and so many other relics that fill the museums of Europe reached France, England, and Ireland.

As Juan García Atienza and Fernando Sánchez Dragó have demonstrated, the Tartessus-Atlantean influence filled the Iberian Peninsula not only with metallic objects and the techniques for crafting them, but also with magical customs, rites, and particularly a mentality that was governed by the fantastic. In those far places, technology, commerce, and religion in no way rejected the esoteric.

100

The Greeks of Marseilles

According to Adolf Schulten in *Maritime Gold* by Avienus, a Roman patriarch and poet, some Greeks from Marseilles sailed around the entire Western Coast of Europe, as the trading treaty signed between Romans and Carthaginians in 500 BC had closed the Mediterranean to Greek ships. The record could not be more descriptive, and the first part is almost comparable to a geographical report:

The description begins at the 'Columns of the North', continuously under threat from hurricanes. The departure points were the island of Quessant and Brittany, precisely the places where the Tartessians searched for the tin they needed for their work. From this point, the Marseillan travellers descended to the Bay of Biscay, which was linked by a land route to Marseilles. It could be said that it was the Marseillans who discovered the isthmus of the Pyrenees between Spain and Gaul. The journey continued round the Cape of Venus (Cape Higuer) and the splendid 'Arabic Headland' (Cape Ortega). They also bordered the 'Island of Saturn' (Berlenga), where it was said an anthropophagic divinity lived, and which was famous for its huge reefs and tall plants. Then they turned the 'Cempos Headland' (Cape Roca) and entered the island of the Tagus, united to Tartessus and Mainake by a strip of land. In this area lived the Cynetes that Herodotus named as the world's most western population. The Marseillan sailors continued their journey along the estuary of Sado and the 'Promontory of the Cynetes' (Cape of Saint Vincent), where there lived a flesh-eating divinity like the one who lived in neighbouring Sagres and gave the place its name of Sagrado. In the Bay of Huelva, covered with mists, appeared the mouth of the Anas (Guadiana). The River Tinto was then called Iberus, because it marked the border between the Cynetes and the Iberians, who from that point extended almost as far as the Rhone. On the hill of la Rábida, there was a temple to the underworld goddess, and there they erected the city of Erbi, which gave the Tinto its name of infernal river ('palus arebea'). At the river began the outskirts of Tartessus, which reached to the wide mouth of the present day Guadalquivir. The River Tartessus then had two streams. The western stream, which must have run to Torre del Oro, has since dried up. The island formed by the two streams was called Cartere and was the Erytheia of Greek mythology. The red dunes that are seen today between Huelva and the Guadalquivir already existed in those times. The highest, Asperillo (328 feet), was called Mount Cassius, an ancient name relating to Kassiteros or tin. Now the Marseillan sailors were approaching the city of silver. They saw the two signs that indicated the entrance: to the west of the mouth of the river Tartessus, a temple; to the east, the fortress of Geron (in the hollow of Saldadina). The ship from Massalia entered the wide river and continued toward the city, which was not far from the sea, opposite Sanlucar de Barrameda.

The last description of Tartessus

In Tartessus, the Marseillan travellers gathered varied information about the river, its course, the neighbouring peoples. The source of the Tartessus was in the mountain of silver, and near to the delta it crossed the lake Ligureo – to the south of Coria – and divided into three branches, further on becoming four. The Marseillans passed before Cádiz, without naming it, but they cited the oracle of the Venus Marina on the island of San Sebastian and wrote of the Phocensian colony of Mainake and the 'Nomnatic gulf' – 'the port of Cartagena'. The Cape of Palos was then called Trete, meaning perforated, due to the hundreds of caves that can still be seen in its cliffs. The journey continued to describing the Mediterranean coast in minute detail until reaching Massalia (Marseilles), the home of the travellers.

Filled with valuable details, the voyage is of great importance for our purposes, as it offers the last authentic and direct description of Tartessus, before the city was destroyed by the Carthaginians. In the year 537, the Phocenses lost their maritime monopoly, which was taken over by the Carthaginians. The ships of Carthage must have appeared at Mainake and Tartessus around the year 530, closing the straits to the Greeks. The people of Mainake opened an over-land pass via Ronda to Tartessus, and Carthage responded by destroying Mainake. Not content with the monopoly of the Tartessus market, they wanted to dominate the whole area and exploit the mines for themselves. In other words, their aim was to annihilate the ancient city of silver, which had been the focus of Western culture and had spread its fame across the whole world. The destruction of Tartessus probably took place around the year 550, and the last eyewitnesses of the Tartessian splendour were undoubtedly the Marseilles sailors who wrote of the foregoing voyage.

The Straits remained closed

Once the city had been destroyed, Carthage took over the entire Tartessian Empire, which included all of Andalusia as far as Cape Nao. In the year 348, when Rome and Carthage concluded their second trading treaty, all foreigners were forbidden to enter the waters south of Mastia (Cartagena). Carthage controlled the straits and therefore the whole ocean. They sent two expeditions in recognition of the fact, one under command of Hannon, which followed the west coast of Africa. The other was led by Himilikon, who sailed north in search of tin and amber. Hannon's voyage has been preserved in Greek translation, but of Himilikon's journey, only a few fragments remain.

Once the straits were closed, the 'Columns of Hercules' became the Non plus ultra of the Greeks: the symbol of the unattainable. Pindarus refers to them in this sense as many as four times, in descriptions of bottomless depths, dense fogs, strong winds and long calms, sea monsters, and whales. And if such omens did not deter the Greeks, the Carthaginians sank any audacious ship that ventured into those waters. Until the Roman conquest of Spain in 200 BC, the straits remained closed. And the cunning Semites guarded their secret of the tin until the Roman conquest of Brittany.

Tartessus is Atlantis

In this way, geographic science was denied further advancement and progress. The exact knowledge of ancient times was lost little by little under a veil of hundreds of fables and fantasies, which converted the Far West into a remote and mysterious land, legendary and enveloped by unknown waters, beyond the Columns of Hercules. The beautiful tale of Atlantis that Plato narrates in the Critias *and the* Timaeus *refers undoubtedly to Tartessus. The fabulous land has been searched for in all places: in America and in Spitzberg, but nobody has thought to look in Tartessus, probably because Tartessus lay in the mists of oblivion. But in fact, the similarities between Atlantis and Tartessus are so numerous that they cannot be put down to coincidence. Atlantis, like Tartessus, was an island near Cádiz, rich in metal deposits, a feature that no other country exploits as well as Tartessus.*

Alongside the industry and commerce in Tartessus, agriculture also flourished. The valley of the Guadalquivir today offers the most favourable conditions for harvesting. One king of Tartessus was, according to legend, the inventor of agriculture, and another discovered bee-keeping. The oxen of Geron sparked the rage of Hercules; the pink wool of the Turdetanian sheep was world famous; and oriental ships brought olive growing to Tartessus.

Thus Tartessus was one of the richest cities of those times. We could represent it as grand and lavish, with stores stacked full of their own merchandise and that imported from other lands. The constant communication with the East must have familiarised the Tartessians with Oriental architecture and technology. The aspect of the city was indeed very similar to a commercial metropolis of the East. On the river, which served as a port, were anchored a large number of ships, and the shores were crowded with workshops and deposits, as described by Plato in his famous poetic work.

Spiritual culture was also very present alongside the material wealth. The Tartessians possessed ancient chronicles and epics, laws written in verse, and everything was written from centuries before in their own language. This is principally what opened the great abyss between the Tartessians and the barbaric Iberians, who never had their own literature. Such an advanced culture in such remote times cannot be explained, unless Tartessus were a colony of merchants or did not at least have long-established close relations with the Eastern Mediterranean. Their writings, above all, suggest foreign influences or, on the other hand, could be a transformation of Cretan literature, for example. If only we could discover remains of Tartessian inscriptions!

The Tartessian Empire

Tartessian art is totally unknown to us, but it is likely that relations with the East favoured its development. Maybe its artwork sleeps, buried under the sand, awaiting discovery, as did Knossos and Phaistos.

The Tartessian state was well organised. Since the beginning of memory, it was governed by its kings, some of whom we

Figure 16. Some pieces of the famous 'Treasure of Villena', Alicante.

know, such as King Gerion (the Geryon of the Greeks) and Arganthonios, the friend of the Phocenses. Tartessus also appears to have had aristocracy formed by the important traders and farmers. The people: villagers, sailors, and manual workers must have been independent.

The Tartessian Empire was extensive. It was the only political civilisation of significance that managed to establish itself in the old Iberia. The Tartessian Empire included all of Andalusia, as far as its natural limits: the sea and the Sierra Morena. It is most likely that this empire was conquered a stage at a time by the city people, whose warlike activity then waned as a consequence of their riches and luxurious style of living. The Tartessians were in fact conquered by the Tyrians and the Carthaginians.

Who were the Tartessians really?

The Tartessians adored the moon. An island opposite Mainake was consecrated to the nocturnal goddess, and they also appear to have made sacrifices to the planet Venus in the sanctuary of Lux Divina at Ebora, near the mouth of the Guadalquivir. And we can also mention the worship of the sun, as in ancient cults these three stars formed a type of sacred trinity. Tartessian religion probably came from the East or from Babylon. There was no shortage of temples, such as Plato describes in Atlantis. The temple that the authors of the Marseilles voyage located on the north side of the estuary was perhaps identical to the temple dedicated to Venus. The kings also were worshipped as gods and boasted of their divine blood.

Daring sailors and busy merchants, the Tartessians were more similar to the Carthaginians than the Iberians, whose worst fault was a limitless indolence. The Tartessians welcomed the Tyrians and the Greeks, not with the blunt condescendence of barbarians but with the prudent liberality of traders, who knows how to sow benefits in order to reap appreciation. All this presents an ancient civilisation of established culture, with flourishing industries, trade and agriculture; a civilisation that was able to unite all the tribes of southern Europe into a vast empire and was wise enough to offer hospitality and courtesy to *other lands, but which was incapable of resisting the attack of conquerors. These features are an exact contradiction of the Iberian people, who instead of cities and wide territories, were divided into a thousand tribes and fortresses; instead of well-organised states, they enjoyed an anarchic freedom; where the Tartessians had commerce, industry, literature and art, the Iberians had nothing but contempt for such things. Instead of benevolent hospitality toward foreigners, they had a warlike barbarianism, which in the mountain tribes was almost bestial. If the Tartessians really were Iberians, it was in no more than name. But even supposing that they were not Iberians, but Ligurians, this still does not explain their ancient culture, as the later Ligurians were no less barbarous than the Iberians. What about communications with the East? Possible, but they would have to have been so constant and so close that they were capable of creating a civilised culture from a barbaric people, something that is difficult to believe.*

So much left to discover

There really only exists one plausible hypothesis: the Tartessians were a colony established by the ancestors of the Tyrians. It is worth considering the Cretans. In the year 1500, culture and maritime strength were flourishing in Crete, and in this period Tartessus was already in existence. Industry, commerce, and navigation constituted the vital aspects of both Crete and Tartessus. Tartessus was a great city, as were Knossos and Phaistos; Tartessus was a monarchy, as was the reign of Minus; Tartessus possessed an ancient alphabet, as did Crete, which in the year 2000 BC already had written characters. And if the Tartessian characters were not indigenous, as it appears, where did they come from if not from Crete, the only maritime power of that time? And lastly, in Crete the worship of the stars and the cult of the bull were widespread.

But if Tartessus was a colony of Eastern sailors, it is evident that its inhabitants were the dominant minority, something similar to the English in India when this was considered the 'jewel of the colonial crown'. The populations of the surrounding territories continued to be Iberians. A small number of conquerors could not have converted the indigenous peoples into Tartessians. But the cultural influence must have been very strong, as only in this way can the superiority of the Turdetanians over the other Iberians be explained.

Tartessus presents us with an important problem, not only for Spain, but also for the East in its traditional relations with the West. The solution of the numerous doubts that still exist, supplementation of the scant knowledge that we currently possess, will only be achieved when we have discovered the remains of the ancient city, and we must do everything in our power to find it.

The most surprising technology

An exhaustive study of archaeological material found in the lands occupied by Tartessus have left one thing plainly in evidence: the surprising level of technology of their craftwork, whether it be jewellery, tools, sculptures, ceramics, or any other artistic profession. For example, it has been proved that painters used tools similar to a pair of compasses and a ruler, as the geometric precision they achieved would not be possible free-hand.

Another astounding discovery has shown that their mechanical materials were worked with lathes, which leads us to assume that Tartessian artisans had learned from the Egyptians, or the other way round, as we already know that in the Nile Valley similar wheels were used to work with stone. However, according to the studies of Petrie and Baker, we know that they used cutting implements that were 'a hundred times' harder than diamond, with which they were able to craft metal containers as though they were porcelain. These tools could not be improved on by any modern technology.

The fact that Tartessian artisans worked with tools similar to pantographs, and that their lathes were fitted with gears and blades, which permitted the precise cutting of pieces, accurate to a hundredth of a inch, could easily lead to the belief that all this is an exaggeration. But it has all been proven by archaeologists.

The term 'high technology' applied to Tartessus has its most convincing proof in the famous 'Treasure of Villena', found in Alicante in 1963. The treasure consists of 67 pieces and 28 bracelets. The first group includes containers, bowls, and decanters of gold and silver, with a total weight of 22 pounds of gold and 2.2 pounds of silver. All the bracelets have unusual forms, but they are identical to the last tenth of a inch, which gives the idea that they were 'mass produced', using a single sheet of gold, neither soldered nor joined. The various pieces of potter are also perfectly identical, which leads us to conclude that the 'repetition' technique was known in those remote times.

We must not leave out another discovery made in the Sevillian village of Lebrija, where six pieces made from single sheet of gold 0.02 inches thick, all absolutely identical.

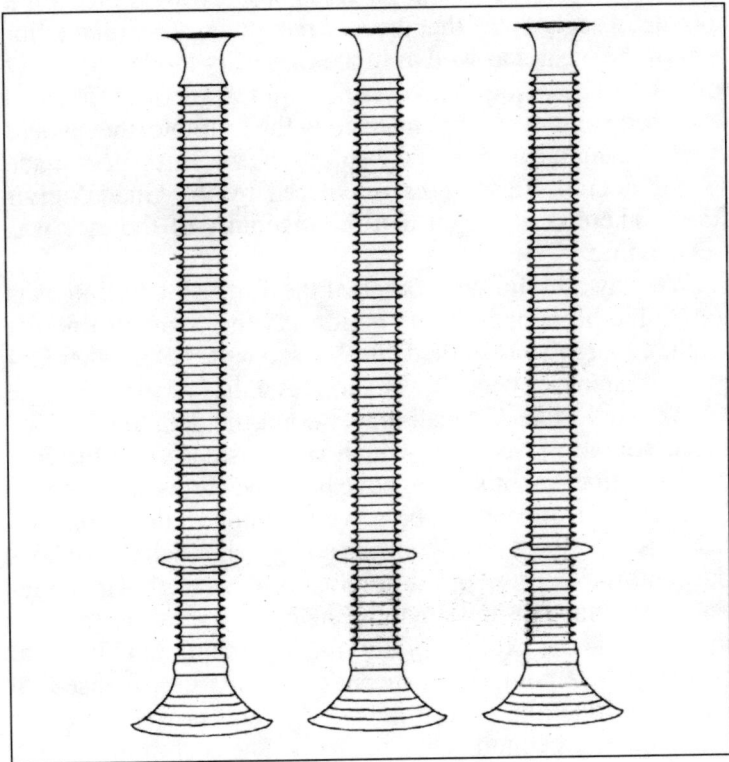

Figure 17. We can appreciate the precise artistic craftwork of the 'Candlesticks of Lebrija' (Seville).

The pieces are 27 inches high and 6 inches wide at the base, and they are decorated along the length of the stem with 44 parallel rings that end at the top. They are hollow and were called candlesticks, though we know that this was not their purpose. They were made with a lathe on a mould, from which the piece was removed afterwards. From a close examination of the pieces, they would seem to have been products of our modern industry.

The Tartessian Rings

A further technological peculiarity can be observed in the 'Tartessian Rings', as the precious stone was jointed on a spindle in such a way that it could remain in place on the fingers of the wearer as well as in the case. Any modern jeweller knows that to achieve this result requires very complicated craftwork, and in attempting to copy the example, they would surely be unable to rival the result of the ancient pieces made by the ancient Tartessians who lived by the Guadalquivir River. There is no doubt that the ingenuity of the race was outstanding.

We may add, furthermore, that the Tartessian writing was a syllabic-alphabetic combination, as the Spanish linguist Gómez Moreno has studied. Strabo also writes of another language system, of which few examples exist.

We would like to recall at this point the detailed work of Professor Adolf Schulten, which we consider to be the best evidence that Atlantis could have been the Tartessian Empire. Moreover, it appears to be a well-founded allegation that leads us to suspect that Spain has concealed much throughout the centuries because of the dominance of a religion and governments that rejected anything heterodox, despite the fact that it was at the expense of burying an exceptional historical period. But of course, this meant conceding importance to a pagan civilisation, whose knowledge and power were not achieved by 'recommended' methods. The best thing to do is continue our journey through the visions that we do have of Atlantis, as we owe it to these enigmas.

Figure 18. Atlantis represented as a sphere which contains all the magical values.

Chapter IX

THERA, CRETE, AND ATLANTIS

When Thera erupted

The island of Thera is located in the Aegean Sea and forms part of the Ciclades archipelago. It is known that in ancient times it measured more than 9 miles in diameter and in the middle towered a volcano over 99.41 miles high. Before it exploded in the most fabulous eruption of all those in the Mediterranean, this small community produced a good wine and must have contained some splendid landscapes, as it was named Kalliste, or 'beautiful island'. It is also known to have been called Strongulê, or 'circular island'.

The amazing eruptions that destroyed the island and the entire archipelago took place between 1500 and 1470 BC. Historians believe that it caused an explosion comparable with that of an atomic bomb in the depths of the centre of Thera. Huge trenches were ripped open in the seabed and especially on the largest island. Enormous masses of stones and ash were hurled for several miles around, and the land was totally altered by being buried in smoke, lava, and flames. The destruction was so complete that since then, the islands of Thera, Therasia, Nea Kameni, and Palea Kameni have been given the name of 'burned islands'.

All have continued to suffer the scourge of eruptions until today, although separated by long periods of time, sometimes lasting more than two or three centuries. We mention it here, because the cataclysm that transformed the islands can be compared to the events of Atlantis. In the study of cataclysm in its essence, it has to be considered as the best example.

An examination of the events on Krakatoa

The volcano Krakatoa presents so many similarities with the explosion of Thera that the information we possess about the development and effects of its eruption is crucial to our understanding of the events of the Lower Bronze Age in the Aegean Sea.

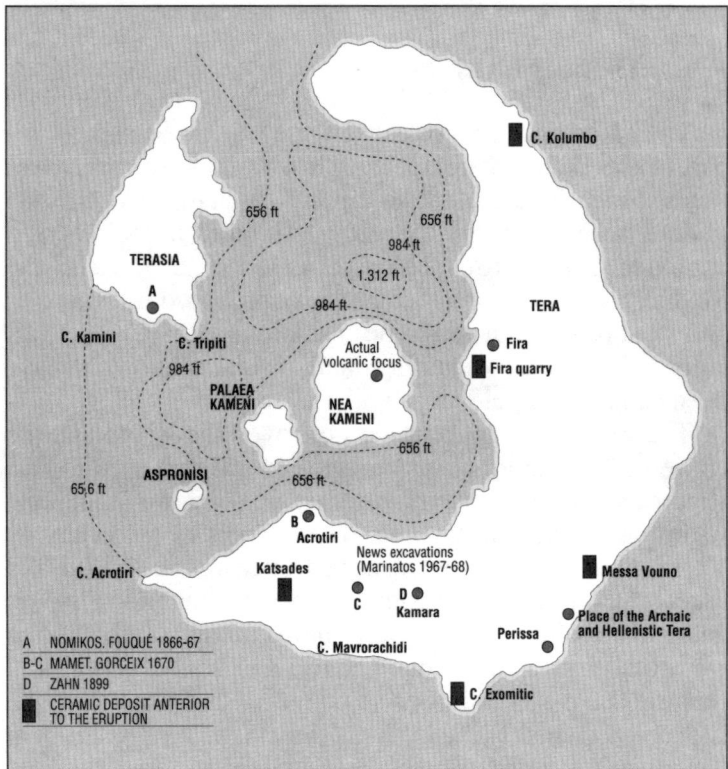

Figure 19. Map of the archipelago of Thera that indicates different archaeological excavations.

The most fabulous volcanic eruption of the last centuries took place in 1883. Krakatoa is also an island that forms part of a small archipelago located in the Straits of Sonda, close to Java and Sumatra along the sea route that connects the China Sea to the Indian Ocean.

The eruption of 1883 did not occur suddenly, as during the six or seven years previous, a series of earthquakes of increasing violence took place, the worst of which were felt in Australia. In 1838, the volcano had already produced a relatively small eruption, though the roar could still be heard 90 miles away, and the ash and dust covered an area of sea extending over some 300 miles.

An expedition that dared to visit the island found it covered in so much volcanic dust, it seemed as though snow covered the entire island. All the trees had lost their leaves from the impact of tons of pumice stone vomited from the crater. However, as the depth of the debris was less than a 3 feet, it was possible to climb to the cone of Perboewatan, where they found a crater some 2,952 feet deep and 147.63 feet across. There is no doubt that the people there were very brave, because a thick smoke continued to come out of the crater, accompanied by rumblings that shook the ground where they stood, and moreover the volcano had not ceased to produce a series of small explosions.

For some years, the volcano remained peaceful, until it exploded again in a paroxysm that produced its most tragic moment on 26th and 27th August. Three ships that were sailing in the area witnessed the event. The Great Cataclysm began with a wave of black smoke that was blown 16 miles into the sky, followed by explosions that were heard 19 miles away. The eruption was spewing pumice stone into the air, which at seven o'clock in the evening was *like an immense pine tree, with the trunk and branches made out of volcanic lights.*

Krakatoa had arrived at the paroxysmal phase of the eruption. Giant waves of over 131.23 feet tall swept the sea, the thunder was heard 3,000 miles away, half the island disappeared beneath the fire spread by the flow of lava and the tremors, and the whole sea was convulsing. It is calculated that the crater erupted over 11 cubic miles of material. The other islands of the archipelago were devastated. At half past ten the following morning, it seemed that the sky had closed in, and the heat and the smell of sulphur and burnt earth were asphyxiating. All ships were forced to seek shelter in the nearest ports.

The windows in houses over 100 miles away were broken by the tremors, and the waves became so high and violent that whole villages were swallowed up, such as Sirik and Anjer, and hundreds of beaches had their physiognomy forever altered. The gunboat *Berouw* was dragged almost 2 miles inland over earth and left 29.5 feet above sea level. And the worst is that 36,382 people lost their lives.

A comparison of the two eruptions

J. V. Luce offered a comparison of the two explosions in his book *The End of Atlantis*:

We know what happened in Krakatoa over a period of 24 hours, and we have plentiful evidence to suppose that the eruption of Thera reached its climax in the same way. A study of the rifts (graben) of both craters reveals a set of similar occurrences with deep openings that form straight lines and follow the principal fault lines. Each crater is generally divided into two basins by a lower crest, and the interior contours of these basins are not different, but Thera reaches a maximum depth considerably greater (1,312 feet to 885.8 feet). Moreover, the area bordered by the walls of the crater is in Thera four times greater than the surface of the sunken part of Krakatoa (51 cubic miles to 14.25 cubic miles). This does not lead to the conclusion that has been repeatedly deduced, that the eruption of Thera was four times greater. However, the shape of the crater and the extension of the deposits of pumice stone indicate that it was at least as powerful as that of Krakatoa, judging by the great depth of the rifts. We know that the deposits of tephra fall in Thera spread over an area of 188 square miles, especially in a south-westerly direction. There are also certain indications that a tidal wave of more than 656 feet in height engulfed the neighbouring village of Anafi. The investigation must be widened, but what we already know leads us to believe that the eruption effected nearby islands, particularly, Crete. Personally I do not doubt that both were highly devastating. If the walls were cracked by the vibrations in the air 100 miles away from Krakatoa, the upper floors of mud bricks in the high palaces and mansions on Crete could have suffered greatly from the same cause. None of the main centres of central Crete is more than 100 miles from Thera. If waves of 49 and 98 feet devastated the beaches of the Straits of Sonda, what effect would be produced along the Cretan coast when an area of land four times greater, at least, than Krakatoa, was sunk in the sea of Thera? More than 36,000 people perished in 24 hours in Java and Sumatra, and 290 villages were destroyed. We do not know what happened in Crete, nor on the islands and coasts of the Aegean Sea, but I believe we can imagine that the loss of lives and material damage would have been no less. They could have been much more significant. I would go so far as to contend that Crete was no longer a maritime power in the middle of the fifteenth century BC. Is it not therefore reasonable to suppose that the eruption of Thera was a determining factor of its fall?

Plato's confusion

J. V. Luce believes that Plato was mistaken in placing Atlantis so far, when most of his story corresponds to Crete. The temples, the peoples, the importance of the island and its commercial and material power relate it to that area. Its destruction by the volcanic eruption that devastated Thera and then produced the tidal waves and tremors put an end to the Cretan empire centred on the island. Phyllips Young Forsyth is perhaps more explicit on the subject, and here we summarise his detailed observations.

Crete and Atlantis are two large islands, and both allow access to a nearby continent. They both fought against Greece and had fertile plains surrounded by mountains close to the sea. In Crete, the fertile lands of Mesara were noted with proportions of 300 × 200 furlongs, which is not far removed from what Plato tells us of Atlantis.

The beauty of the mountains of the mythical continent can be compared to that of the Cretan landscape, where the mountains range from a height of 4,752 to 8,038 feet. Another similarity is that both islands possess valuable and plentiful sources of differ-

117

ent kinds of wood, and if those of Crete no longer exist today, we know that in ancient times, this island was covered in fir trees, maples, oaks, planes, cedars, and a great variety of abundant low brushland and pasture, which served to fatten herds of cattle.

We find further coinciding factors in the agriculture of the two islands. Plato's Atlantis employed an irrigation system that allowed it to reap two harvests a year: one in winter and another in summer. The first benefited from frequent rainfall, while the second was supported by the skilful construction of channels. The same system was used in the valleys of Crete, where grapes, olives, and a variety of cereals were grown.

Thanks to agricultural production and wide trading, the islands were probably inhabited by a large population. Crete was made of some three hundred centres of population, the main one being Knossos, where 30,000 people lived, although in its times of greatest prosperity, that figure was tripled. Archaeologists raise the number of inhabitants of the whole island to 250,000, which is close to the number given by Plato for the population of Atlantis.

The similarities continue

The mining of ores and their smelting, and the skills of their artisans are other factors that Atlantis and ancient Crete have in common. Their mines gave gold, silver, and other metals, and from their quarries were excavated white, red, and black stone. Egyptian and Greek historians have proved that ships frequently left Cretan ports loaded with finely crafted metalwork, which was easily sold wherever the ship was bound.

With regard to the political situation, the systems of the islands are so similar, they could be described as mirror images. Both were formed of ten political constituencies, as Knossos had been constructed on a hill, from whose slopes the palace controlled the governments of Phaistos, Mallia, Zacros, and the rest. However, each of the governments had a certain autonomy.

King Minos' palace was similar to the one described by Plato. It must have been so splendid that even today its remains inspire admiration at their suggestion of past lavishness. Moreover, the ruins found allow us to form a fair idea of the riches that it must have held. One of the most surprising similarities consists of the sacrifice of bulls in the temples. The form of capturing the animals with nets, of jumping over them as a game, and afterwards their death with a sacred knife is the same. The whole process has been recorded on glasses, statues, and seals. In fact, the legend of the Minotaur sprang up in Crete.

The importance that the people attached to columns is obvious on both islands. They both worshipped Poseidon, and they shared flora and fauna, but on Crete there were no elephants, only lions. Many of the animal species have disappeared with time, but modern Crete is still much richer than continental Greece in flora, possessing more than 139 species of native plants.

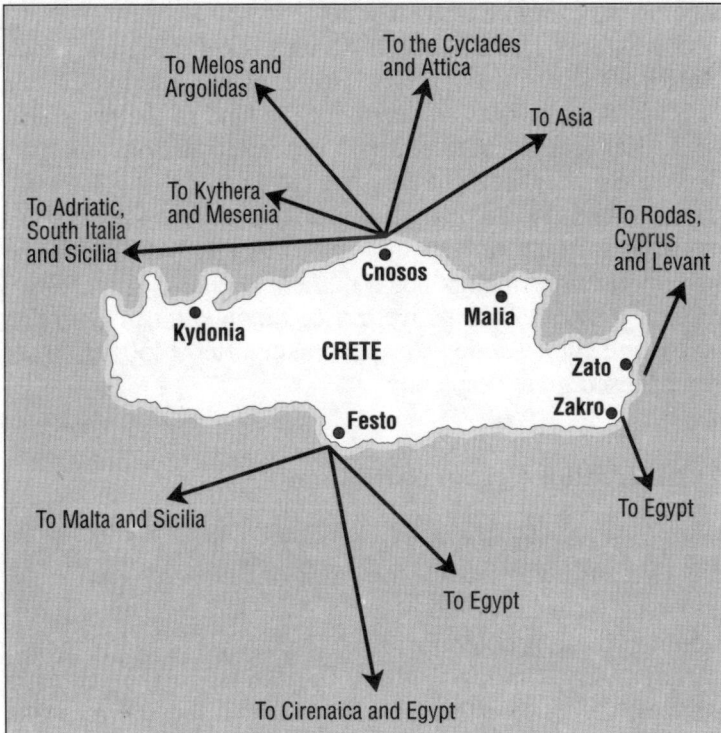

Figure 20. The principal routes for the trade Crete maintained with all its neighbours.

The most important coincidences

Another two points in the argument for the similarities between Atlantis and Crete must be made in that both islands suffered a catastrophic event. The former was devastated by earthquakes and floods in a single day and night, and the latter seems to have met a similar fate at the eruption of Mount Thera. It is believed that the tremors and the 'tsunami' tidal waves wreaked devastation on Crete in around 1450 BC, while Plato affirms that it became difficult to sail in the waters of Atlantis after the disaster, which could be due to the quantities of pumice stone that must have remained floating in the Cretan Sea long after Thera had been submerged, a phenomenon that has been documented with sufficient accuracy by the example of Krakatoa.

Lastly, it is clear that both Atlantis and Crete maintained close links with ancient Egypt. However, considering the tale of Plato, Atlantis was an enemy of the land of the pyramids, while Egypt and Crete enjoyed peaceful relations, and the two were physical neighbours. We have proof that much trading went on between them. It is probable that the Cretan ships made an infinite number of trips to Egypt, with which the two civilisations maintained a mutually beneficial exchange. In fact, the Cretan ships were a common sight in Egyptian ports, and their sudden disappearance after 1450 BC must have caused great perplexity.

The incredible Cretan civilisation

On an examination of the technological advancement of the Cretans, we find factors that have been verified by archaeological excavations, and we are left with the impression that these people must have lived in a kind of paradise, perhaps very similar to that of Atlantis. In the fantastic palaces, there were the highest comforts and services that humanity would be ignorant of until the end of the nineteenth century or our era. We should never forget that we are discussing the years close to 1700 BC.

The chambers of important people were arranged around a central patio, which contained gardens and fountains. The walls were double, to guard against cold and keep cool in summer and, for the same reason, were decorated with mosaics, painted with everyday scenes. The floors were covered with tiles and fitted with a kind of aquarium where beautiful plants grew and a wide variety of fish lived. The water was fed with a stream of air through small pipes so the fish could survive.

On the upper floors of the grander houses, there was running water and flushing lavatory systems. There was also an air-conditioning system built with stones and metal, which was fed by a central heating system that in summer provided cool air. The people also had a sewer and water supply system, as well as hydraulic lifting appliances that worked by inertia. Another of the wonderful luxuries was a lighting system used in the rooms at night and in underground or enclosed areas.

The streets were paved with slabs and, in some cases, concrete. The houses were separated by alleyways and paths 150 cm wide, but there were raised pavements for pedestrians. The roadways were constructed on a slope, so that the water would be channelled to the centre when it rained.

After 1900 BC, the Cretans founded cities such as Akrotiri and those that occupied Santorini, the present name for Thera. Homer wrote that the cities of Crete numbered over one hundred. During the first period the urban population was centred on the West Coast, and later Knossos and Phaistos were built almost in the very centre, the former in the North and the latter in the South.

The volcanoes started to erupt around 1700 BC, but the Cretans continued to build new palaces, and worst of all, a rivalry sprouted between the most important cities, until the Great Cataclysm of the fifteenth century BC. It could have been due to volcanic activity, as we have described, which calls the situation in Atlantis to mind, particularly for the speed at which the whole thing took place: a single day and night.

Some doubts exist

...To affirm that ancient Crete and Thera were the only prototypes for Plato's Atlantis does not seem completely justified, given the evidence. From Crete, Plato could have derived the concept of an island suddenly destroyed by a violent act of Nature; memories of ancient Crete, Egypt, and Greece have preserved certain knowledge of the political system, geographic characteristics, natural resources, and religion of the island. Moreover, the passing of time since the Bronze Age until the Classic Period easily could explain the confusion, especially with respect to dates and sizes.

And there are still characteristics of Atlantis that certainly are not reflected in ancient Crete. For example, where on Crete can we find the parallel of the concentric rings of land and sea that are fundamental to Plato's island? And where in Crete are there temples similar to that of Poseidon: of a stadium 90m long and plated on the outside with silver, with golden figures on the pediment and ivory tiles on the roof? The Greek temples, of course, were a far cry from ancient Crete, where simple relics, arranged normally in a palace or in a private house, served for worshipping the deities. In reality, it was only after the Bronze Age that the architectural form of the Greek temple was configured.

In the same way, there is no parallel in ancient Crete of the stone wall of Atlantis, with towers and gates. As Sir Arthur Evans noted during the excavation of Knossos, the Cretan palace was unusual in the ancient world precisely for its lack of fortifications. Moreover, many minor characteristics of Atlantis, such as the public baths and race tracks, have absolutely no equal in Crete.

Therefore, even if Crete had served as the 'principal' model for Atlantis, it was a 'limited' model. Plato clearly mixed characteristics derived from other sources. In other words, his Atlantis was a combination, a mixture of different elements. Some of these elements must have been totally created by his imagination; others however, he took from external inspiration, from his own experiences as a cultured man of the world.

As we can see, the path in search of the answer to the enigma has reached a stage of 'possibility', which does not block the path, as we still have many other pieces of evidence to investigate. Some of them may be a little far-fetched, and we will even deal with others that are rather debatable, but what is most important to us is not to leave a single stone unturned.

Figure 21. The art of Minoan Crete gave us this painting of 'The Happy Prince', who was perhaps an inhabitant of Atlantis in the Aegean Sea.

Chapter X

THE MAPS OF PIRI REIS

An exceptional find

The maps drawn by Piri Reis form part of those documents buried in the world's libraries, left at the mercy of termites, dust, and rats. Cataloguing and archiving systems have be subject to inconsistent changes over the years. Baskets of documents donated to the king or the nobleman of the time were stored without being opened, as he had just died, and his heir was still not clear due to disputes between his legitimate and illegitimate children, when no more complicated situations arose. As such, many documents that reached libraries were stored without being catalogued.

In umpteen cases, losses have resulted from fires, transfers, or other incidents that impeded the exact recording of the contents in the general deposits. Malil Edhem, director of the Turkish National Museums, tried to correct this situation – a huge task for the employees of the Topkapi library in Istanbul, where millions of handwritten and printed manuscripts are stored, some of which are unique for their rarity and historical value. If we also bear in mind that Turkey was one of the most important empires of the Mediterranean for nearly six centuries, we can imagine the quantity and quality of the documents that must be stored in the library-museum of Topkapi.

It is known that on 9th November 1929, two world maps were found there that were thought to have been lost: those drawn by Piri Reis, which are thought to date back to earlier than 1523. However, they must have been considered important documents, as they were preserved in a special place after being catalogued, and no further work was carried out on them. Their existence remained recorded, even if only in memory.

Who was Piri Reis?

The name of this Turkish sailor or pirate was Piri Muhyi 'I Din Re'is. He appears to have been born in Gelibolu, a port of Dardanelles. Those were the times of the glory of Mohammed II, 'The Conqueror', who took Constantinople from the Christians. His date of birth is not known, but we have some idea of the year of his death, as he was beheaded on the order of Solomon 'The Magnificent' in 1555. He was accused of running the ship that he was commanding aground.

Pierre Duval wrote that he reached the rank of 'kapurdan', or admiral, in Egypt, due to his great knowledge of the sea, both in cartography and naval strategy. He defeated many Christian ships at sea and carried out many raids on ports and cities in different parts of the Mediterranean, mostly to capture slaves.

Piri Reis is said to have received a map from his uncle, Kemal Reis, that had belonged to Christopher Columbus himself. The map had been found on a Christian prisoner who had served under Christopher Columbus many years before. Piri Reis writes in the 'Inscription V' dedicated to the 'Western Sea' (as the Atlantic was known for many years) of his 'Bahriye', a work that the cultured class of Turkey valued as one of the most important of the time:

A certain unbeliever, who was called Columbus and was said to have been born in Genoa, was the discoverer of new lands. To do this, he must have used a book that told him that beyond the Western Sea, to the West, there were coasts and islands where rich metals and precious stones could be found. After careful study of the book, he devoted himself to begging the important people of Genoa for help, saying "Give me ships so I may go there and dis-

126

cover these lands." But they answered him: "Be quiet, dreamer! How can you think that the Western Sea has limits? Has nobody told you that it ends in thick fog and unending night?"

So Columbus decided that he was wasting his time with the Genoese and went to the King of Spain, to explain his idea to him in full detail. There he received a similar response, but he begged so much and was so insistent, that the King gave in and gave him ships, well-equipped, and said to him before he departed: "Columbus, if what you have said to me is true, I will name you Governor of those lands!" And so Columbus set sail for the Western Sea...

This text may perhaps give the idea that Piri Reis was rather simple, at least in his writing. However, this could not be further from the truth. He knew all the languages of the Mediterranean: Turkish, Greek, Italian, Spanish, Catalan, and Portuguese. As a polyglot, he was able to make the most of all the maps and books that came into his hands, and thus he explains how he made his own:

...Nobody possesses such a high quality map. I used some twenty maps of Mappae Mundi, drawn in the times of Alexander the Great, the lord of the Two Horns, and marking the inhabited areas of the world. We call them Zaferiye. I also used a Hind map and others made by four Portuguese sailors, who had sailed the Western Sea to the south to reach China, which were drawn geometrically. I have also made use of a map drawn by Columbus, representing the western region. After reducing all these maps to the same scale, I have reached this final layout...

Piri Reis also spoke with sailors who had sailed to the New World, all of whom shared secrets their secrets with him with the idea of forming a good ally, since they were all prisoners or slaves. It must be remembered that in those times, almost all the Mediterranean was under the dominion of the Turkish fleets, and battles and raids were common.

A gift that sparked the imagination

Only fragments of Piri Reis' maps have been preserved, which means we are unable to see the whole of the Atlantic Ocean and the American, European, African, and Antarctic coastlines. It was all drawn on coloured parchment paper and included an infinite number of illustrations, including portraits of the kings of Portugal, Morocco, and Guinea. In the African continent, an elephant and an ostrich illustrate the map; in America, there are llamas and pumas; in the ocean and around the coasts, ships are drawn; and birds decorate the islands. The texts are in Turkish. The rivers and mountains are drawn in profile. The colours used are employed in a singular manner, for example, the rocky areas are shaded in black; sandy and shallow seas are marked with red dots; and currents hidden beneath the sea are marked with crosses.

Those who contemplated the map in 1929 may have just seen a fallen empire, and for this reason the map was simply stored away like all old documents. But they should have brought the find to the attention of other specialists, as several libraries from other countries also requested copies, which were also kept.

We had to wait until 1953, when a Turkish naval officer sent a gift to his friend Arlington H. Mallery, chief engineer

Figure 22. The map of Piri Reis is the oldest map of America, which also shows Atlantis, situated in the Antarctic.

in the Hydrographic Office of the United States Marines. He was an intelligent and imaginative person, who had already published a book called *Lost America*, in which he demonstrated that there existed an iron culture in the New World before the Spanish invaded, with details using radiocarbon and firsthand witness accounts. He also followed traces of the Vikings to verify whether the Norwegian language had exerted any influence on the Indian tribes that lived in Canada.

But fame was to reach Arlington via the gift he received, as he consulted several specialists in ancient cartography and set himself to make a painstaking study of the map. He did this in response to a professional instinct, based on the more than five years that he had spent on researching and writing his book. He left no stone unturned, for he was convinced that all his evidence should be supported by solid documentation and respected professional opinions.

He went to only the best, amongst whom we should mention I. Walters, a famous cartographer, and R. O. Linehan, an expert on polar matters. However, he would have achieved nothing without the aid of the Swedish explorer Nordenskjöld, who took eighteen years to transcribe, or interpret, the language and the signs of the map. To help him, he used modern trigonometry from 1970.

What the map shows us

In his book *The Atlantis of Piri Reis*, Manuel Gómez Márquez writes the following:

...At the beginning of the sixteenth century, the map of America was still unknown by European sailors. The same surprise, if not greater, was created by the discovery of the Canary Islands and the Azores, as these islands had been considered an integral part of a larger island that had only existed in the imagination of a few investigators, who founded their visions of Atlantis as a great island on faith.

After long investigations, Mallery and Walters concluded that Piri Reis had either not used the usual coordinates of

129

his time, or that he had known that the Earth was round, and his maps were drawn accordingly. This only left the two investigators still more perplexed, and they decided to carry out more thorough research. They produced a type of grid with which they could read all the details and dimensions of the ancient map, and transfer it to a modern globe of the Earth. At this point, they were amazed. Not only did the contours of the American coast, but also those of Antarctica match up exactly with those that we know today with the help of modern science.

In the world map of Piri Reis, we can observe that the South American point of Tierra del Fuego extends in a thin strip that almost unites the land with Antarctica, where it widens. In the present day, this area is beneath the sea and is frequently ravaged by violent storms, where sailing conditions are very difficult even for large and heavy ships.

The map of Piri Reis was compared inch by inch with the profiles of the submerged land obtained with the most modern techniques: aerial photography, underwater pictures taken by infra-red cameras, acoustic probes transmitted from vessels, etc. All this went to prove that, indeed, some 12,000 years ago, there did exist this continental bridge between South America and Antarctica. Piri Reis's representation of Antarctica shows meticulous and exact profiles of coasts, bays, and headlands that can no longer be appreciated, due to the thick layer of ice that covers them.

The coastlines of Antarctica must have been copied before the continent was left covered in ice. In this region, the ice is almost a mile thick. We do not have any idea how these details could appear in a map only according to the geometric knowledge that was available in 1513.

However, the map of Piri Reis shows us the coastline of Antarctica and even indicates the height of mountains that are currently hidden by glaciers, some of which were not even studied until 1958, in the International Geography Year.

The maps of Piri Reis have been compared with the most modern examples, and the differences are minimal.

130

Faced with this strange situation, the point of view expressed by Professor Charles H. Hapgod is totally logical:

The evidence offered by the ancient maps suggests the existence – in remote times and before the birth of any known culture – of an authentic, relatively advanced civilisation that was situated in an area and maintained trading relations with the rest of the world, something like a universal culture.

Given this evidence, we cannot deny the fact that the maps used by Piri Reis must have been drawn by a civilisation that existed some 12,000 years ago or more and that had arrived at the same level of development as where we find ourselves today.

We must bear in mind that Piri Reis and his map do not only show an unfrozen Antarctica, as America, Europe, and Greenland also appear with no ice. This shows that the level of the seas and oceans was lower than that of the present day and leads us to the conclusion that the last glacialisation (Würn) took place after the Great Flood, which was possibly caused by a large amount of artificial rain, suggesting that the maps used by Piri Reis were therefore drawn before the Flood.

If we accept the world map of Piri Reis as a map drawn on the basis of harbour charts (possibly) or geographical maps from the period before the Great Flood, we therefore must also accept that Atlantis was a fact.

We must take the Phoenicians into consideration

At the end of the sixties, Russian scientists came to the conclusion that the maps of Piri Reis did not correspond to Antarctica, but to the south of Patagonia and Tierra del Fuego. This assertion, however, is questionable, as these two territories were unknown until the arrival of the Spanish conquerors in the year 1520.

What leaves no doubt is that Piri Reis had details prior to those of Christopher Columbus. Some historians have thought that he could have obtained such information from

Viking maps. However, the Vikings only covered the coasts of part of North America, where they established a type of port for storage of provisions or small colonies. It is known that they made many journeys during a period of warm weather, which had reduced the ice of the North Pole and the presence of icebergs, but we know nothing of any maps they made, especially of places they never visited.

In the search for intrepid travellers who may have been in America often enough to elaborate maps, which later could have been used by Piri Reis, the most pertinent is to head for the Phoenicians. We know that these people had ships that were capable of crossing the Mediterranean in any season and against strong tides. However, the crossing of the Atlantic would require something more, as it would have meant more than a month at sea. Of course, humankind's daring has never known limits.

It is also possible to imagine Phoenician sailors lost at sea, who reached 'with great effort and thanks to benevolent conditions the American coast'. Moreover, they were able to return to tell the tale, which encouraged others to follow their adventures. It is certain that many perished at sea, while others achieved the crossing and returned alive. This helped to construct the legend of the Middle Ages about a mythical continent that existed beyond the Western Sea.

Columbus' biographers have told us that he had mysterious maps to guide him, which perhaps are kept in the libraries of Portugal or other places, and which drove him to think that that there was a different route by which to reach the Indies. It is written that Saint Isodore confirmed in the sixth century that *another continent exists, apart from the three that we know, on the far side of the ocean, and there the sun is warmer than in our regions.* In the fourteenth century, the legend was told of the Breton monks and how they went to sea to extend evangelism to the West, as they were convinced that on the far side of the Western Sea there existed other lands. But their destiny is unknown, as they never returned.

We have evidence, some of which was obtained by Professor Stolks, that the Phoenicians were in America. What is strange is that the Phoenicians did not record their discoveries when they maintained trading relations with the whole of the Mediterranean. But we also know that many records have been intentionally erased from history, because they were not convenient to the powers that be of the time.

Motives to fire the imagination

The specialist Arlington H. Mallory writes about the maps of Piri Reis: *in the times when the maps were made, something more than the existence of a few extraordinary discoverers was needed, since it was essential to have hydrographic specialists who were both very competent and well-organised, as it is impossible to trace the maps of continents or areas as large as Greenland, Antarctica, or America, which was apparently achieved thousands of years ago. This task would have been impossible for a single person or a small group of explorers. To accomplish it, practically a whole society of astronomers, cartographers, and other technicians are needed, something which was only possible in a civilisation that was accustomed to making use of such knowledge. It is difficult to imagine how this map could have been drawn without the aid of aviation. We must consider that the longitudes are exact, something that we have only been able to achieve since little less than two centuries ago.*

What Arlington Mallery is suggesting is that we should revise our idea of history, because as we continue to carry out archaeological excavations, penetrate into the most secret depths of libraries, and find methods of deciphering hieroglyphics and other complicated writings, we are becoming more and more aware that there existed civilisations, such as Egypt, that accumulated knowledge far superior to that of other civilisations existing at that time.

In *The Rebellion of the Wizards*, Louis Pauwels and Jacques Bergier reveal a surprising discovery that 'fires the imagination':

Arlington M. Mallery, a specialist in pre-Columbian America who has made notable discoveries within this field, was searching for a great vanished civilisation that had existed on the American continent. He was able to present a series of elements, some of which were disconcerting, especially furnaces for working with iron – the dates of which the specialists cannot agree on – and some stones bearing inscriptions. This discovery was made in Pennsylvania, to the east of Harrisburg, in the house of the Strong brothers. The specialists that Mallery consulted – Sir W. M. Petrie, Sir Arthur J. Evans, and J. L. Myres – found certain resemblances in these inscriptions, perhaps Phoenician or perhaps Cretan. The inscriptions seemed to correspond to a phase prior to the first Mediterranean writings, as they marked the start of alphabetisation, but the writing, which is not really syllabic, contains as many as 170 signs and still has not been deciphered.

Arlington H. Mallery believes that the writing is from an earlier ancient American civilisation, prior, naturally, to the known pre-Columbian civilisations (Inca, Maya, or Aztec). These civilisations probably would bear some traces of an earlier people, and in this way such phenomena could be explained, such as the mysterious fortress of Tiahuanaco, whose date had proved impossible to fix, as well as certain peculiarities of Mayan astronomy, which appears to refer to a sky many millenniums older than the one we know, and the strange legends of ancient civilisations, etc.

But even if we recognise the existence of such a civilisation in the American continent 10,000 years ago, we would still have to explain how their geographical knowledge reached Europe.

And as we have cleared the boundaries of reason, we can give free rein to fantasy: what if this advanced civilisation existed not only in America, but on all the Earth?

Could such a civilisation have an extraterrestrial origin? With regard to the maps of Piri Reis, it would be difficult to implicate beings from Venus or other planets: because if, as is to be supposed, they had advanced rockets, why did they need to make a detailed map, not of the Continents – which would be more easily explained – but of the coasts and shorelines? This, of course, does not mean that it is not worth studying the question, but the maps of Piri Reis are maps exclusively for sailors from this planet.

So could they have been inhabitants of Atlantis or of Gondwana? But the movement of the continents has a history that goes back more than ten thousand years, and the time we are interested in and these Continents, if they existed, had disappeared or been converted into rubble a long time before.

We can assume, therefore, that one part of the human race that coexisted with other less-developed peoples, attained eight or ten thousand years ago a high level of civilisation, which included a thorough knowledge of the planet and that was destroyed by a great cataclysm. Charles H. Hapgod is convinced of his conclusions. Only a century ago did we start to push back the limits of history and discover material traces of civilisations that had been considered mere myths (Troy and Crete) or completely unknown (Sumer, the Hittites, the Valley of the Indus). Hapgod declares that we must continue our studies, and that they must be strongly directed toward the discovery of the advanced civilisation that existed more than ten thousand years ago. Naturally, we leave the responsibility of these affirmations to him, which, we must stress, have been backed up by painstaking scientific investigation. The greatest archaeological discovery is yet to be made...

There is no need to hurry. Better to take our time and make the true discovery of the location of Atlantis. For the moment, we simply note that the maps of Piri Reis provide further evidence that the mythical continent was located in Antarctica.

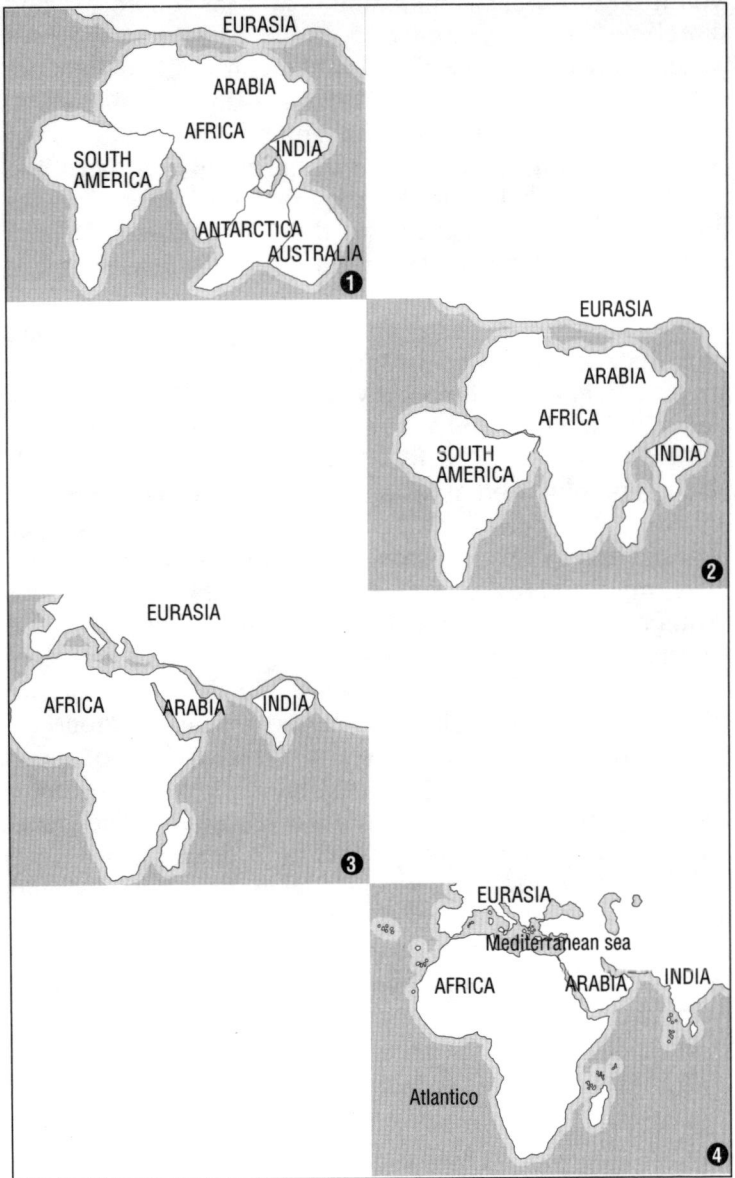

Figure 23. The movement of the continents, according to the theories
of Wegener, showing the formation of the Atlantic Ocean and the
Mediterranean.

Chapter XI

TIAHUANACO, A SEA PORT IN THE ANDES

Hoerbiger's theories

We must travel to the Andes, find Lake Titicaca, and adjust ourselves to the purity of the oxygen, for we find ourselves at 13,123 feet above sea level. In this region, the natives take the leaves of the coca bush and other plants to adapt to the climate, which moreover is marvellous. But this does not stop us being surprised, even amazed, at the existence of Tiahuanaco: monumental ruins of great stones, some of which weigh almost eight tons, which form a temple that constitutes one of the greatest enigmas of humanity.

Simply by turning to the theories of Hoerbiger, it is possible to explain the existence of this monumental complex, though his theories are only an approximation. Thus we must accept that thousands of years ago, one of the Earth's several satellites changed its course, that the moon may have been the third, prior to the current one. This change of course provoked such alterations on Earth that the continents started to separate, and above all, the sea level descended more then 9,842 feet. This fact must be remembered when we are describing the mysteries that surround Tiahuanaco. In the first place, we have been able to verify as certain the existence of a surface of marine sediments that covers an area of some 450 miles. This surface begins near Lake Umayo, in Peru, some 328 feet higher than the level of Lake Titicaca, and ends beyond Lake Coipousa, 820 feet from its northern end. All this proves that in this area, which at no time has had a flat surface, there was a sea.

The geologists who support the Hoerbiger theories believe that the tertiary moon absorbed the sea water, therefore transporting it to this height, where it remained for enough time to leave the sediments found. This process must have taken place some 250,000 or 300,000 years ago. One of the shores of the sea must have reached the point at which, today, we find the ruins of Tiahuanaco, which must have been a sea port at the end of the Tertiary era.

Figure 24. A diagram of the mythical character who appears at the entrance of Tiahuanaco.

Who built Tiahuanaco?

The civilisation that lived in this area of the Andes has not been found in any other part of America. Investigators place it in the year 4000 BC, when the Egypt of the pyramids was already showing signs of a great culture. With regard to Tiahuanaco, the architects that designed the city used enormous stones, whose surfaces were carved by mysterious scribes. The designs also include great stones in the doorways, measuring 9.8 feet tall and 1.6 feet thick, which were sculpted with chisels to create astonishing images. Together, this group weighs more than ten tons. But some of the stones of the great wall weigh as much as sixty tons, and the blocks that support the walls have a weight of up to a hundred tons.

If we add to that the presence of fabulous statues, whose weight is enormous, the only conclusion we can draw is that Tiahuanaco was built by giants, human beings of unimaginable size, who were capable of moving these huge blocks of stone around the mountains – brothers of the race who filled Easter Island with its famous statues. However, why was such huge architecture designed to house men and women of normal size, no taller than us?

The proven existence of giants

Some ancient cultures believed we were taught the arts by a race of god-king-giants. The great megalithic masses that cover many areas of the Earth bear witness to such characters. The Bible also mentions Palestinian tribes who had giants as kings, and there are many investigators who relate the statues of Easter Island with the work of giants. One giant was the god Osiris, who taught the Egyptians the techniques of sculpture, and for this reason a statue was made that gave credit to his exceptional size.

There is evidence that in Titicaca, the royal castes were giants, who were the first to be put to work, whether carrying stones or designing new buildings. With them were men and women of normal size, according to our current proportions,

139

who considered themselves fortunate to have giants who governed and instructed them.

A port of cultured people

The port of Tiahuanaco was salt water, as is the water in Lake Titicaca. This points to the disappearance of a vanished ocean. The ruins of the walls of the entire complex also still exist. Hoerbiger believes that the sea covered the Andes mountain range, the great peaks of Mexico, and part of Tibet. Half the world's legends mention that the water reached an inconceivable height, which gave form to the story of the Great Flood. Amongst the myths of the Mediterranean, there is one that tells of giants who descended from the fifth peak of Abyssinia.

Using our imagination, without making the task seem like a crazy fantasy, we can see the ships from Tiahuanaco travelling all over the world. The elements that support this possibility can be found in the most ancient traditions of Greece, the region of Yucatan, the African tribes, and in the heart of Asia.

The proof that a cultured civilisation existed in the Andes is given by a stone calendar, which was deciphered in 1937. It was found buried in dry lime and broken into two parts, though its ten-ton weight prevented the sections from separating. The archaeologist Ponnansky was the first to study the document, to fix the solstices and the equinoxes. The German professor Kiss was able to read the weeks and the months, and the English scholar Ashton completed the study of the symbols, which revealed the totality of elements of this scientific testimony. One of them was that the calendar of Tiahuanaco consisted of 290 days.

In 1927, Hoerbiger reached the conclusion that in the Tertiary age the Earth took 298 days to travel around the Sun. Moreover, each of these days lasted twenty nine of our current hours. The Viennese scientist died in 1931, and all his reports are filed in the institute that bears his name.

As Tiahuanaco must have been built some 50,000 to 100,000 years ago at the end of the Tertiary age, the duration of the Earth's journey around the sun is a coinciding factor. We are talking about a calendar that started in the autumn equinox of the southern hemisphere and was divided into four parts, separated in the middle by the solstices and equinoxes that marked the astronomical seasons of the year. Each of these was divided into three sections, containing twelve parts. We could go on with the details to demonstrate the scientific quality of the calendar, which is of a surprising level given that the calendar is more than 4,000 years old, and it was found in the American Andes!

The highest sculptural art

Few civilisations in the world have been able to make an artistic offering of such high quality as that found in one of the main statues of Tiahuanaco, which the Spanish called *El Fraile*. The statue gives a sense of peace and great wisdom, as the image is very stylised and has a rare equilibrium. Its face is composed of geometric forms: the eyes are circular, the nose a pyramid, the mouth an oval, the forehead a rectangle, and the profile has the form of a fragment of an eclipse, to which an added straight line would give form to the head. About these sculptures Bellamy wrote:

The sculpted heads have high foreheads, open faces, expressive profiles, forthright chins. In a particular way the head – probably that of a dignitary, as it is covered with the official cap – is unforgettable. It seems to emerge from the stone in which it is sculpted, for it is not completely finished, as though the impatience of the sculptor's chisel was telling us that it is incapable of finishing the work, because its grandeur proves too much for it...

At this point, we ought to underline the differences that existed between the colossi of Tiahuanaco and the Easter Island statues, for the former show the superior intellect of their creators. Their mastery of the art is so great that it is difficult to believe such results could have been achieved in such remote times. However, the sculptors who created the statues of Easter Island were too simplistic, though the statues reach giant proportions.

Gods who teach

Most primitive civilisations are linked to the memory of powerful gods, who shared an existence with humans to instruct them in agriculture, metallurgy, and the sciences. In general, happiness reigned during this period, thanks to the beneficial dominion of these all-powerful beings. The Greeks remember a time, called the era of Saturn, that preceded the terrible conflicts between the giants and the gods. This did not stop the memory of Hercules being associated with feelings of gratitude, as also happened with the Titan Prometheus.

The Egyptians and Mesopotamians based their legends on the god-kings, to whom they owed their culture and their progress as superior beings. The indigenous peoples of some of the Pacific tribes talk of giant ancestors who created the world. This encourages the idea that there were times in which a paradisiacal Atlantis did exist, enjoyed by many nations, until ambition shattered the harmony that would lead to self-destruction.

The end of Tiahuanaco

After an examination of the ruins of Tiahuanaco, we can guess its destruction. It could have happened between 10,000 or 12,000 BC (some date it closer to 250,000 BC). While the tertiary moon wobbled on its course around the Earth, the oceans were shaken by great convulsions. Volcanoes erupted, and the ground was wrenched apart by an infinite number of earthquakes.

Around Lake Titicaca, evident signs of different catastrophes have been found: stratums of volcanic ash, deposits from flash floods, and lastly, signals of the disappearance of the sea. There is a zone that is startling in its evidence, in which colossal, half-sculpted stones are found, as though the

142

artisans working on them were surprised by something that forced them to leave as fast as possible. The tools excavated from the lime give an idea of the chaos that ruled.

When the satellite struck the Earth, it flattened everything in its path, and when the cataclysm finally subsided, the sea returned to a level that was not much higher than that of today, as the force of the moon was gone. The atmosphere also suffered alteration, to the extent that the inhabitants of the region of Titicaca were left defenceless. They were 13,123 feet above sea level. The ships that had been the principal method of transport were totally destroyed by the apocalyptic tidal wave that preceded the disappearance of the sea, and they were left without food.

All the human beings who had inhabited paradise in the American Atlantis had to fashion a new existence. Many did not succeeding in overcoming the change, while those who did survive had to learn everything afresh as if they were orphans. They were reduced almost to primitive beings. However, some of them were unwilling to forget the past and left evidence; others set out to various points around the continent, to the regions of Yucatan and Mexico. Some of them would form the Mayan and Olmec civilisations.

Nobody has explained this situation better than Plato, though it is impossible to affirm for certain to whom he was actually referring:

They and their descendants found themselves deprived for generations of the most common necessities of living, which forced them to concentrate all their intelligence on the simple task of satisfying their most immediate material needs.

When humans were left defenceless

We must assume that what took place in Tiahuanaco was also experienced in Abyssinia, New Guinea, Mexico, Tibet, and other places all over the world. We could also include events that gave birth to legends, such as the Great Flood, though with more evidence than only the word of the Bible.

However, before the events of the Great Cataclysm, humanity had become vain. As the people had lived at the side of the gods, in an almost fraternal relationship, they ended up considering themselves equal. They fought with the gods and then amongst themselves. Death and sin became the passport to achieving power. Moral decline reached the limits of the utmost degradation. Then the events that Plato writes about in Atlantis occurred: *the gods were so horrified by the crimes of humankind that they decided to punish them.*

But can we believe that they were the cause of the fall of the Tertiary moon, something which must have happened gradually, over a period of thousands of millions of years? It must have been something less cosmic, though superior to all previously known tragedies. Humans were left defenceless and had to learn to live under new and very different conditions, as precarious as living in caves. But this did not mean that some of them could not leave evidence of their past, be it through legends, statues, or other methods.

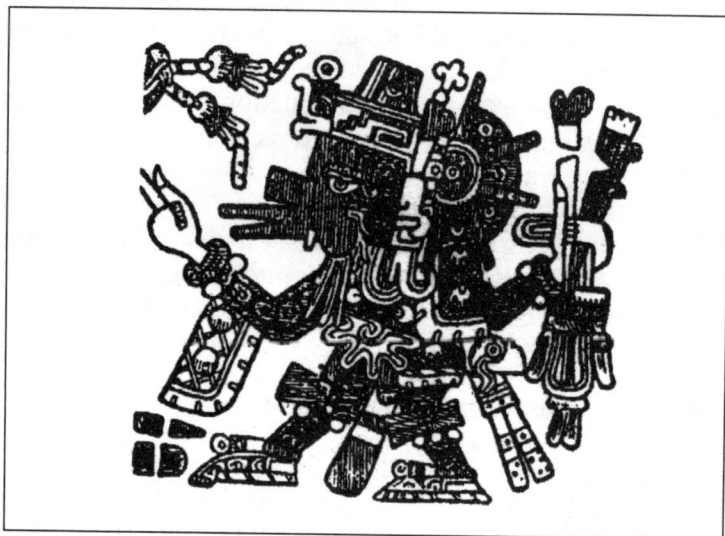

Figure 25. The god Quetzalcoatl of the Toltec people (according to the Florentine codex).

The Toltecs of Mexico

The Toltecs lived in ancient Mexico, on one of the large islands that existed during the Tertiary age. Of these people, we only know what is told by Spanish records and, above all, through what has been discovered by current investigators, such as G. C. Vaillant, who writes in *The Aztecs of Mexico*:

The eastern history of the Toltecs was written by Ixtlilxochitl. As is to be expected, it starts with the creation of the world and passes through four or five eras, referred to as suns.

The first era – the Sun of the Water – began when the supreme god Tloco Nahuac created the world; after 1,716 years, floods and thunder destroyed it.

The second era – the Sun of the Earth – saw the Earth populated by giants, the Quinametzinos, who disappeared almost entirely when tremors destroyed the Earth.

The third era was the Sun of the Wind, when the Olmecs and the Xicalancas, races of humans, lived on the Earth. They killed the surviving giants, founded Cholula, and spread as far as Tabasco. A miraculous person, called Quetzalcoatl by some and Huemac by others, appeared in this era and taught civilisation and morals to humankind. When he saw that the people did not want to receive his teachings, he returned to the East, after predicting the destruction of the world by storms and the metamorphosis of humankind into monkeys, all of which came to pass.

The fourth era is our day, called the Sun of Fire, and will end in general conflict.

We can draw a scientific frame around all the above in the style of Hoerbiger . We also would have to include the geological stages: the first era prior to humankind; the second era with the creation of the giants; the third era with normal men and women co-existing with the giants; and the fourth era, which is our era, in which no giants remain; the arrival of good giants, such as Quetzalcoatl, and the degeneration of the human race (converted into monkeys from the instant the king-god leaves after realising his advice is unwanted); the moral motive for the Great Cataclysm; and all that we have told until now.

Some details about the great events were preserved in Mexico:

In the divine catastrophe, which ended in the Flood, Xelhua and his six brothers, the entire race of the giants, saved themselves by taking refuge on the peak of a high mountain, which they consecrated to Tlaloc, the god of water. To celebrate their survival and show their gratitude to the god, and also to have a shelter in case of a further need, Xelhua built a zacuali, *which was a tall tower that reached to the sky. But the gods were offended by this show of pride and launched the fire of the heavens on the work. The workers perished, and this is the reason why the pyramid of Cholula remains unfinished.*

Figure 26. Colossal statues at the Temple of Tula in Mexico, called the 'Atlanteans'.

We can see that there are no end of links between giants and the mountains, even found in the legends of western cultures, for they represent symbols of superiority or the dream that humanity wishes to recover: the protection of the gods found at the highest summits.

Apart from this surprising legend, we have very little knowledge of the Toltecs, but the evidence they bear is that they were related in some way to the American Atlantis, demonstrated by their mythology.

Chapter XII

THE GREAT VISIONARY OF ATLANTIS

A mother's will

A person's size, origin, or hair colour are unimportant if he or she has the creative impulse of a dreamer of impossible goals, but knows how to present them as tangible realities. In this way, it is possible to create a 'great visionary'. A purpose that the parents of Ignatius Loyola Donnelly certainly never imagined when they brought him into the world in Philadelphia in 1834.

Their home was a humble one, though not ignorant. His father had been born in Ireland and became a priest, until he hung up his habit to become a shopkeeper and study medicine. His wife was also an active woman and skilled at finances, as she acted as a money-lender: four dollars given on Monday were converted into five by Sunday. It seems that her clients, all housewives, must have paid their debts religiously, as the profits she made paid for her husband to become a doctor.

Unfortunately, he did not have much time to enjoy his new profession, as after two years he was infected with typhus by one of his patients and died in hospital a few days later. His wife was six months pregnant at the time. She gave her husband the best burial and a respectful funeral and devoted herself to her children. She never married again, though she was an attractive woman and did not want for suitors.

She was kept busy with the care of her children, including two daughters who said of their mother with affection: "I don't know how her glasses don't break with the terrible look she gives us when she thinks we've done something bad." She was a strict woman, but never struck her children, not even a slap. Despite the continuous housework and the money-lending business, in addition to the long hours she spent at night with her accountancy books, she always found time to help her children with their studies.

A shadowy future

We can see that Ignatius L. Donnelly had a firm base to enable him to achieve the best qualifications at High School, where he received several literary prizes. He was a short, red-haired man and could not be said to be handsome, but he had a way with words, and that added to his talent for improvisation helped him to become a lawyer. As soon as he finished his university studies, he started work as an articled clerk.

Three years later, helped by the support of his mother, he began his own practice, and almost at the same time he became involved in politics, using his conviction, his ability to communicate with people according to his social position, and his knowledge of the general problems of society. Senator John C. Breckinridge is known to have congratulated him personally.

However, young Donnelly had fixed his sights on the West, which at that time was the aim of many North Americans. He went on a series of journeys before he made up his mind to move and bid farewell to his mother in 1856. He and his wife arrived in Minnesota, where he and an associate intended to transform a simple town into a true city, which they called Niningir City. He also continued to be involved in the Republican Party.

Niningir City turned out to be an impossible fantasy, which Donnelly abandoned as soon as he established himself as a successful orator. It is possible that he did not want to be linked with failure, especially after he took up the position of Vice-Governor of the State. Three years later, he arrived in Washington as a congressman and retained the seat in the following election. However, the civil war was to cut his political career short.

He was a determined man and stood as a candidate for the Democratic Party, but did not obtain the post. He believed that he had been the victim of foul play and spent years fighting to reveal the truth. But in the end, he was forced to admit defeat.

The greatest library about Atlantis

Ignatius L. Donnelly accumulated a small fortune, having inherited his mother's money sense and being married to a woman of few needs. We have mentioned that he had obtained literary prizes at school, and he always wrote his own speeches and collaborated with the press. In this way, he became a popular figure.

He was also a great fan of the novel, history books, and essays. His passions included archaeology and geology, and he previously had participated in several excavations in Philadelphia. His biographers say that during his stay in Washington, he was a regular visitor to the Library of Congress, which had one of the best literary selections in the country.

One day in 1870, he discovered Jules Verne's novel *Twenty Thousand Leagues Under the Sea*, which he read with great delight. And as soon as the crew of the *Nautilus* discovered the remains of Atlantis, he became engrossed in the subject and started to collect books about the lost continent.

Ten years later, he was surrounded by the best library in existence about Atlantis. He had read all the books, essays, articles, and studies that he could and decided to write his own work, asking his literary associates to help him with the publication of the book.

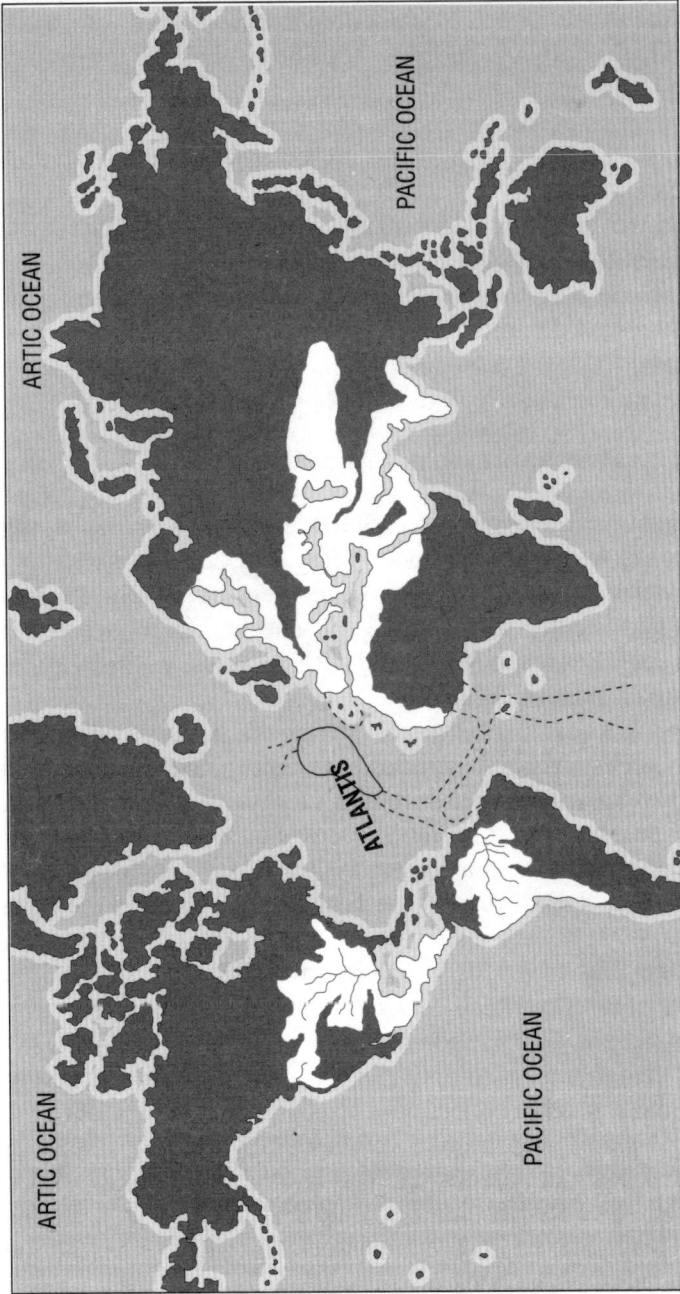

Figure 27. The map suggested by Ignatius L. Donnelly, which situates Atlantis and the areas that it influenced.

The material he used included all the topics related to the lost continent: mythology, geography, world history, ancient literature, etc. He investigated all areas and even introduced issues that touched on superstition, esoteric matters, and the supernatural.

A universe created with documentation

As he wrote, Donnelly became convinced that Plato's Atlantis had existed, and after some months, in 1882, *Atlantis: The Antediluvian World* was published. The work formulated thirteen proposals:

1. That at one time there existed, in the western mouth of the Mediterranean, in the Atlantic Ocean, a great island, which constituted the remains of a continent that the ancients had called Atlantis.

2. That the demonstration of the mentioned island offered by Plato should not be considered a legend, as has been believed for many years, but an authentic account.

3. That Atlantis was the place in which man was first able to surpass his original condition of barbarity and become a civilised being.

4. That, in time, the island became a powerful and populated land. The huge demographic density led to exploratory voyages, which reached the coasts of the Gulf of Mexico, the rivers Mississippi and Amazon, the Pacific coasts of South America, Western Europe and Africa, the Baltic, the Black Sea, and the Caspian Sea, where they established settlements of civilised societies.

5. That it should be considered the authentic antediluvian world and, at the same time, the Garden of Eden; the paradise of the Hesperides; the Elyssian Fields; the Gardens of Alcinus; Olympus; the Asgar of the legends of the remote peoples; and that it represented the common memory of a great land where primitive humanity lived for many centuries in peace and happiness.

6. That the gods and goddesses of the ancient Greeks, Phoenicians, Hindus, and Scandinavians were the kings, queens, and heroes of Atlantis, and that all the events called mythology constitute a muddled compilation of authentic historical events. Because they were taken from the memories of a place that was exceptional.

7. That the mythology of civilisations such as those of Egypt and Peru conceded great importance to the religion that emerged from Atlantis: the worship of the Sun.

8. That the most ancient colony organised by the Atlanteans was probably in Egypt, whose civilisation was almost an exact copy of that which existed on the island.

9. That the most common objects from Europe's Bronze Age originated from Atlantis, and that the Atlanteans were the pioneers of iron work.

10. That the Phoenician alphabet, which engendered all European languages, comes from the one used on the island-continent.

11. That Atlantis was the base land for the origins of all Aryan and Indo-European nations, as well as the Semitic peoples and possibly also the Turanian races.

12. That Atlantis perished due to terrible natural convulsions, which brought about the sinking of the island in the ocean, destroying all its peoples.

13. That no more than a few people were able to escape in various types of vessels, to carry the news of the catastrophe the lands of the east and west, which have reached our times via myths of the Great Flood, which are told by different peoples of the old and new worlds.

As these proposals make clear, Donnelly constructed a solid world around Atlantis based on vast documentation, possibly the greatest that another author has been able to consult. This was one of the causes, together with the direct literary style of the author, that led to the book being re-edited forty-eight times in the United States and twenty-six times in Great Britain. Its success was so resounding, maybe because the public needed to believe in something solid, due to the foundering of many traditional concepts at the end of the nineteenth century, that the author's presence and knowledge was requested in hundreds of international forums. We believe that his success could be considered some sort of 'great vision'.

Another passage from Donnelly's work

It is easier to appreciate the great success of Donnelly's work if we read one of its passages:

Let us suppose that we find the remains of an enormous submerged island in the middle of the Atlantic, facing the Mediterranean and close to the Azores, which measures 1,000 miles wide and between 2,000 and 3,000 miles long. Would this not provide us with the proof of Plato's claim that an island larger than Asia Minor and Libya combined, called Atlantis, existed beyond the Straits and close to the Columns of Hercules? And let us imagine that we discovered that the Azores were the peaks of mountains from this submerged land, devastated and ripped apart by terrible volcanic eruptions, surrounded now by underwater land covered in thick layers of lava and thousands of miles of volcanic debris?

Would we not thus be forced to recognise that these discoveries constitute solid evidence that Plato's account was true; that 'during a tragic day and night, violent earthquakes and floods raged, which caused the disappearance of the powerful nation'? Atlantis was submerged under the waves, and the ocean was converted into an unreachable area, due to the huge quantities of mud and stone that covered the island-continent.

All this has been definitively proved by the latest investigations. Ships of various nationalities have carried out soundings at great depths; the Dolphin, of the United States; the German frigate Grazelle, and the British ships Hydra, Porcupine, and Challenger have drawn a map of the ocean bed, showing a great chain of mountains that stretches from an area of the British Isles to the coast of South America, to Cape Orange, toward the beaches of Africa, and finally to the southeast toward Tristan da Cunha (…) The submerged land (…) is 9,842 feet above the great depths that surround it and emerges from the waves as the Azores, St. Paul's Rocks, Ascension, and Tristan da Cunha.

We are faced with the vertical column of the lost continent, which in remote times occupied the entire Atlantic Ocean and from whose coastlines Europe and America were formed. The deepest areas of the ocean reach 3,500 fathoms and represent the areas that sank first. These are the plains located to the east and west of the central mountain range; several of the highest peaks of this chain, such as the Azores, St. Paul's, Ascension, and Tristan da Cunha, are still above sea level, while most of Atlantis lies at a depth of a few hundred fathoms beneath the surface. This mountain chain shows us the path that once linked the New and Old Worlds, by which the black-skinned races travelled from Africa to America and the red-skinned Indians from America to Africa, and which provided the connection for plants and animals to spread their species throughout both continents.

As I have pointed out, the very same law of nature that initiated the gradual descent of the Atlantic continent and raised the lands on its east and west is still acting. The coast of Greenland, which could be the extreme north of the submerged continent, continues to sink rapidly beneath the water, leaving the old houses built on the low rocky islands currently under water; their inhabitants have learned by their own experience not to build on the shores of the sea. It is possible to observe the same depression along the coast of South Carolina and Georgia, while Northern Europe and the Atlantic coast of South America are rising rapidly. In South America coasts 1,168 miles long with heights ranging from 98,42 to 1,279 above sea level have appeared.

In the times when these mountains extended from Europe and Africa to America, they held back the currents of tropical waters to the north, and the Gulf Stream did not exist. The land contained the ocean, which bathed the shores of Northern Europe and was very cold. The consequence was a long period of glacialisation, and once the barrier formed by Atlantis was sufficiently submerged to allow the natural flow of warm waters from the tropics to the north, the ice and snow that had covered Europe slowly melted; the Gulf Stream

156

flowed around the island-continent and still maintains the circular current that it followed with the existence of Atlantis.

The officers of the Challenger found the surface of the mountain chain to be covered with volcanic debris, the residues of mud that, according to Plato's account, permitted the crossing of the sea after the island's disappearance.

This does not prove that the mountains that linked Africa and America were sunk beneath sea level at the time of the destruction of the island. They may have slipped slowly toward the sea or have been demolished by further catastrophes like those recounted in Central American literature. Plato's Atlantis could have been reduced to the 'Dolphin Range' that we know today.

The North American ship Gettysburg has also made several important discoveries in a nearby area. The discovery of a bank of soundings at the points N 85° O, and at a distance of 130 miles from the Cape of Saint Vincent, announced not long ago by Commander Gorringe on his last Atlantic crossing, could be related to the soundings previously obtained in the same area of the North Atlantic.

The foregoing evidence indicates the probable existence of a platform or underwater chain that connects the island of Madeira with the coast of Portugal and the probable connection of the island, in prehistoric times, with the far southwestern part of Europe.

Sir C. Wyville Thomson proved that examples of the fauna from the Brazilian coast were similar to examples from Southern Europe. This could be explained by the existence of a mountain chain that linked Europe with South America.

The crew of the Challenger found, shortly after their expedition, that the great underwater mountain range was no other than the remains of the lost Atlantis.

Donnelly carried away by enthusiasm

Modern specialists on the subject of Atlantis believe that Donnelly succeeded in sparking the interest of the world, to the point that it was believed that Atlantis had not disappeared. They praise his use of wide-ranging documentation, which allowed him to achieve lofty interpretations of history – for example, that Homer's Phaeacia could have been a memory of the lost continent; however, they regret having to discount all his theories, due to lack of evidence.

For example, the localisation of Atlantis in a specific era is incompatible with the idea that we currently have about the Mesolithic and Neolithic periods, as is the birth of the great cultures in the valleys of the Nile, the Tigris-Euphrates, and the Indus. We could point to an infinite list of facts, like those related to the great Atlantic mountain range, which have been discounted.

We should understand Donnelly, because he started with the idea that there was only one interpretation of Plato's texts: his own. And as the 'great visionary' that he had become, he read the documents that he collected according to this role. If he found something that contradicted his theories, he transformed the information without hesitation, as was the custom in past times. He also used excessive declarations of discoveries with insufficient evidence.

Despite all this, Donnelly's works – for he published more than one on Atlantis – are still being published, which presumes there are still people today who continue to believe his theories. Here we have offered them as one of the many paths leading toward the deciphering of the principal enigma.

A disciple of Donnelly

Lewis Spence is considered Donnelly's disciple, since the publication of his three books on Atlantis in the 1920s. His intention was to give a more scientific base to the theories divulged by his compatriot. First, he attempts to provide geological evidence to sustain the hypothesis that a large mass of land occupied most of the North Atlantic area during the Tertiary age. According to his studies, the Atlantic island-continent was divided into two parts, one of which was Atlantis, situated off the West Coast of Spain, and the other, Antilles, which was located in the current West Indies.

These two islands were stable, as were other smaller islands, during the entire Low Pleistocene era. The Great Cataclysm that submerged Atlantis took place around 10,000 BC, but the Antilles did not suffer such destruction, as can be seen in the numerous islands that currently are found in the Caribbean.

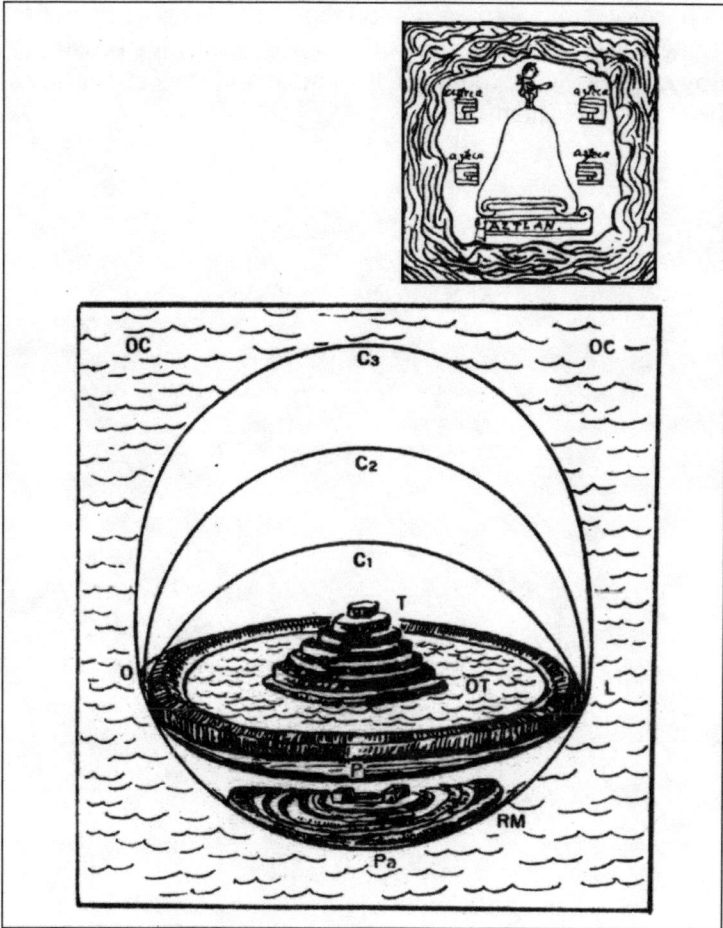

Figure 28. Above: Mayan representation of Aztlan. Below: The Babylonian concept of the world. In the two figures we may observe many coincidences with Plato's description of Atlantis.

159

Thanks to the existence of the island-continents, Spence demonstrates the influence the Atlanteans exercised over Western Europe, Egypt, and the New World during the Stone Age, which resulted in the development of the Mayan civilisation.

The critics have been more favourable to Spence than to Donnelly, as Spence took his sources from well-compared archaeological discoveries and, above all, did not attempt to create a doctrine, but took his stance from the 'possible'. However, his work did not sell as many millions of copies as the ex-Congressman.

Chapter XIII

THE SLEEPING PROPHET AND OTHER DISTURBING CHARACTERS

Treatment diagnosed under hypnosis

Edgar Cayce was born near Hopkinsville, a town in Kentucky, in 1887. He left school before completing even the primary education to work in a bookshop. We know little about his cultural initiation, except that he was already having remarkable experiences when he lost his voice from a throat infection. It is possible that he possessed prior information about man's mental powers.

Before he suffered the illness, he intended to become a priest. His family took him to all the doctors in the area, but to no avail. Then, they took him to the State Capital, and he was admitted to the best hospital, but this proved to be a waste of time and money. However, just when his family was starting to think they would never find a cure, they read an article in the newspaper about a hypnotist who could cure hopeless cases abandoned by conventional medicine.

The Cayce family contacted this person, whose name is unknown and whose 'therapy' may be described as surprising; he put the boy into a hypnotic trance and when he was asleep he asked him about his illness and what the treatment was to cure it. The 'sleeping' boy had never studied medicine, had no knowledge of any kind about medicines and had never witnessed the cure of a mute who previously had the power of speech; yet he described in a clear voice his own diagnosis and the form of applying it. When he was awoken, he still could not speak, but when he followed his own advice, he was cured.

As the event was considered quite amazing, the local press published the news. The doctors had to admit that there was a possibility that somebody could self-diagnose an illness with such assurance that they achieved cure by their own conviction. But what remained unexplainable was how Edgar Cayce had forgotten completely everything he had said while in the trance.

The 'sleeper' who began to cure

Once the impact of his case had been forgotten, Cayce returned to his work in the bookshop, but one of his relatives fell ill soon afterwards. The whole family was very worried, until one night Cayce started to talk in his sleep, but what he was saying was like a kind of repetitive 'lecture'. When his words were eventually noted down, it was revealed to be a list of medicines to be administered to the sick relative, as well as the exact doses and times at which they should be taken. In light of the miracle cure of his voice, the family paid heed to what he said, and the patient recovered. With a second cure, Cayce began to collect more clients. The most surprising is that he could never remember what he had dictated in his sleep and was therefore incapable of understanding how he did it with no knowledge of the subject in question.

Strangely enough, Cayce never wanted to study medicine, nor visited a pharmacy, but in his sleep-diagnoses, he mentioned medications by name, including some that were only about to be put on the market by the pharmaceutical companies, but had never been advertised, and others that had just been withdrawn from the market. But in every case, the patient was cured after following his pharmaceutical recommendations.

People always take advantage

As Cayce never knew what had been asked of him when he awoke, he was warned people sometimes had asked him for the results of a horse race, the numbers of the lottery, or other similar predictions. The realisation that some of his friends and family had tried to obtain personal benefits from his gift, which he did not consider his own but from a higher power, displeased him so that he refused to carry on giving 'sleeping' advice.

Some time before, he had acquired some knowledge of photography, which he had put into practice even though fate seemed to be against him: a fire destroyed his laboratory, and soon after, in his new laboratory, the explosion of a tin of magnesium burnt the eyes of one of his collaborators, Hugh Lynn. When he heard that his friend was going to lose an eye from the accident, he did not hesitate to put himself into a trance, and his friend not only kept the eye, but recovered his sight.

The consequence of this was that the 'seer' returned to his role of medical adviser, but this time with his wife as his assistant, to prevent questions being asked for personal gain. Cayce carried out this role for more than twenty-seven years, at times for application to his own children. Many doctors tried to impede what they called his 'quack doctoring', but they did not effect Cayce's popularity. Edgar Cayce carried out this practice under the name of the Association for Investigation and Illumination, based in Virginia Beach.

The 'lectures' on Atlantis

In 1920, Cayce became interested in metaphysics, owing to the information that his friend Arthur Lammers was collecting. One afternoon, as a game, he decided to tell his friend's horoscope, but once in the trance, he started to tell Lammers not his future, but all about his past lives – the series of people he had been reincarnated into in the past.

163

When Cayce read his wife's notes of what he had said, he was astonished. Just as he knew nothing about medicine, he was completely ignorant in the matters of the occult and reincarnation. At this point, he was bombarded with doubts, as he had always been a devout follower of the Bible.

From that moment on, Cayce behaved differently, because he wanted to find out all he could about the occult, as well as Buddhist and Hindu teachings. This enabled him to offer a different kind of help to the people who consulted him, in addition to the medical treatments.

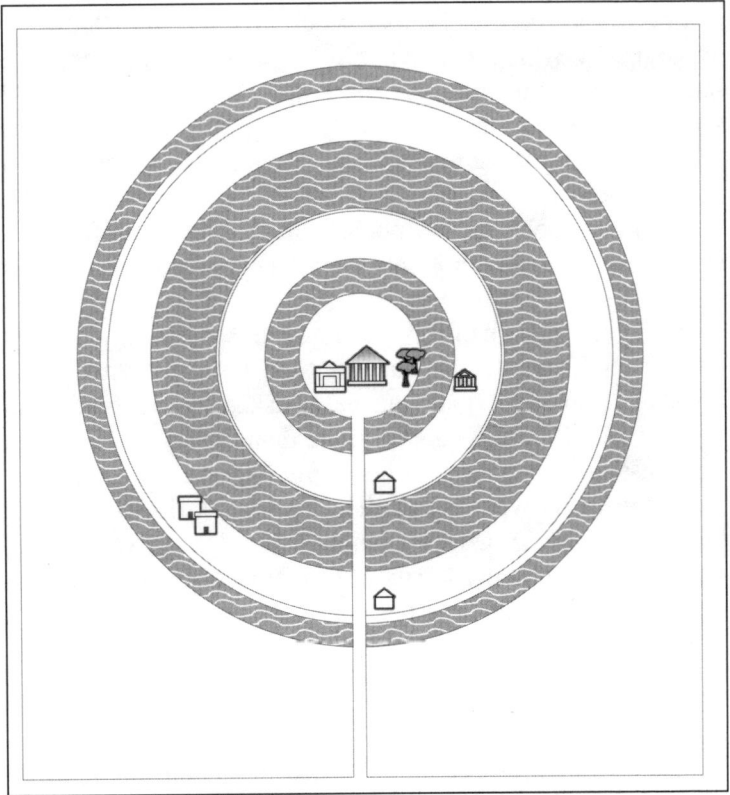

Figure 29. The interior of the city of Atlantis according to Plato's description. It took the form of a giant ring and extended from a mountain through three circumferences of earth and water. An avenue led to the centre of the city.

On the 12th April, 1939, when Cayce was 62, he began to talk of Atlantis in one of his trances. In spite of the fact that his words were not very specific, what he said can be recounted in these sentences:

From the lost island-continent where the land was swallowed up by the ocean waves emerged the civilisation of the Mayas, or what we now know as the Yucatan. The first nation to ply the seas in an airship.

This surprising revelation seemed to be some sort of prophecy and was accompanied by other visions during the following twenty years. What he recounted was closely related to Plato's writings, but also included new information, such as the Atlanteans' possession of extraordinary technical gadgets, many of which did not exist in the twentieth century, such as the 'Stone of Fire':

It had a six-sided form, in which light appeared as a means of communication between the finite and the infinite, or as a means by which combinations were originated with those forces that emit energies, as a centre from which radio activities emanated, which guided the different forms of transitions or voyages during those periods of activity of the powerful Atlanteans.

It had the appearance of a crystal, though very different from the crystals that we know today. Do not confuse the two, therefore, as they are many generations apart. It was in those times when aeroplanes or other methods of transport controlled themselves, even though in those times they were able to travel by air, or by water, or underneath the surface of the water. But the force by which they were governed lay in the power plant, the stone Tuaoi, which was like the beam on which they acted.

In principle, it was the source from which mental and spiritual contact originated.

The 'Stone of Fire' should not be seen as the forerunner of the laser, but as one of the ways that the Atlanteans used to contact the spirit world.

More than 672 of Cayce's 'lectures' on Atlantis have been recorded. In tthese he mentioned men and women who populated the lost continent in previous incarnations, until they were forced to scatter, some on board an aircraft, in order to divulge their great knowledge to the whole world.

The Atlantis that Cayce saw

In 1923, in one of his trances, Cayce said:

The position occupied by the continent of the Atlantis lay between the Gulf of Mexico on the one hand and the Mediterranean on the other.

He continued to specify that the land was the size of a continent and that its people had inhabited the land for thousands of years. During this time, it underwent three catastrophic episodes of destruction, the last of which occurred 11,000 years ago, when the whole continent disappeared.

However, before the Great Cataclysm, the Atlanteans achieved a civilisation that, in a certain way, was similar to the industrialisation of the twentieth century. The people also made up an active and ambitious society, capable of generating electricity and building aircraft. As Cayce said in a trance on 19th April 1938:

The entity is what today would be electronics; that energy or influence was applied to aircraft, ships, and what today we call radio, for both constructive and destructive purposes.

Moreover, Cayce recounted, in rather a confused manner, that the Atlanteans possessed a stone called refractory, which they used to generate electricity. This stone has been compared with the radio active materials used today to produce nuclear energy. As Cayce said in this trance of 1938, more than a decade before the first test of atomic energy:

The preparation of this stone was left only in the hands of the experts of the period; the entity lay among those who controlled the influence of the radiations, which were in the form of rays invisible to the human eye, but which had an effect on stone as driving forces, both when the aircraft was propelled with the petrol of those days or when they were used to drive leisure vehicles that could travel not only on land, but also on the sea or under the waves.

These vehicles were driven by the concentration of rays that came from the stone, which was situated at the centre of a nuclear station.

According to Cayce's words, the Atlanteans came into existence on the Earth as spirits and continued to evolve until they became material beings. This was the cause of their destruction, along with the continent. As they lost their spiritual form, more conflicts arose in the civilisation. In another trance Cayce recounted:

At the moment when these destructive forces were unleashed or before the negative energies were released that caused the first destruction of the continent, the evil could be observed that had been the use of the spiritual in things related to the sensual of the matter.

Therefore the Sons of Belicia took over the government of Atlantis and converted the lower classes, the artisans, and the workers in general into slaves. This was the beginning of the decline of their society, until the great geological cataclysm, combined with an inept use of technology, perhaps because it got out of their control. In 1936 Cayce said:

Figure 30. The British Colonel Percy Harrison Fawcett on his first expedition to Brazil 1908.

In Atlantis, after the second destruction of the Earth, as a result of the misuse of divine law on earthly and natural matters, the eruptions began, starting with the second time they used those influences which were for the development of mankind but turned into destructive forces due to their improper use.

Cayce's account of the existence and destruction of Atlantis included the prediction that the civilisation would resurface during the 1960s near Bimini, a Caribbean island. Years later, in 1968, some divers discovered near Bimini, on the ocean floor, something that resembled a highway, built with rectangular stone blocks. This lead to the belief that Cayce's prophecies had been fulfilled. When the remains were tested with 'Carbon 14', they were calculated to be 12,000 years old.

However, archaeologists have found similar formations in the sea bed around Australia, which cover a surface area of some 4 miles. They concluded the formations were not man-made, but came about naturally during coastal formation with the disintegration of marine creatures that sank to the bottom, forming hard rocks that were then broken or scored, giving them the appearance of great paving stones, due to the sinking of loose sand and the effects of the sun's rays.

This was the explanation given by science, which did not harm Cayce's credibility too much, as after his death, he still had thousands of supporters. His heirs still keep the Association set up by the 'sleeping prophet' very active.

In search of 'City X'

Very few people in the world have as many admirers as jungle explorers. Novels, cinema, and television have turned them into heroes, although they are sometimes presented as visionaries. One such man was the English Colonel Percy Harrison Fawcett. He developed his expertise drawing maps of Ceylon and South America as a young man.

In 1908, he led his first expedition in Brazil and Bolivia. Years later, after retiring from the army, he started on the adventure of his life, in search of a lost city created by the Atlanteans, which he called 'City X'. His desire to achieve this goal was sparked off by a black stone idol, given to him by the writer and adventurer Sir H. Rider-Haggard, author of the fascinating novel 'King Solomon's Mines'.

As Fawcett took the trouble to consult a clairvoyant, he found out from him that the figure came from a continent that stretched from the coasts of Northern Africa to South America, and moreover, he was told that the figure had travelled to the heart of Brazil. The former Colonel believed that he had found the exact place when he bought a map of the Mato Grosso, because it featured a city with no name.

He set off straight away on his voyage, accompanied by his son Jack and his friend Raleigh Rimmel. When they arrived at the Brazilian jungle, he wrote to his wife to say they had heard talk of an ancient city situated on a lake. But nothing further was ever heard of him and his companions.

As usually occurs, a large number of Europeans who visited those places began to hear stories of decrepit ghosts that claimed to be Fawcett, while others swore that they had met children with fair hair and blue eyes, dressed like the indigenous people of the region. There were also those who said that Fawcett and his followers had found his City X and decided never to return, but to stay in the 'paradise created by the Atlanteans'.

The most surprising news was broadcast by radio and the newspapers, that the Irish medium Geraldine Cummins had established mental contact with Fawcett, who had found remains of Atlantis, but who was very ill. Many mass media followed 'these spiritual dialogues with a living being', of which there were four, the last one being in 1948. In fact, the explorer described his own death in that year.

The Russian girl, friend of the hunchbacks

The Russian girl Helen Petrovna looked like a doll, with her long dark hair and blue eyes, but there was nothing doll-like about her character. As a child, she was accompanied by invisible friends, who she affectionately called hunchbacks. She found them in the long corridors of the apparently maze-like cellars of her house.

Another custom she had, was sleepwalking, through which she maintained a double life, divided into day and night. She also had an active imagination, which combined with a talent for words, she used to terrify her school friends with fantastic stories, as a result of which some suffered hallucinations.

Despite the disapproval of her parents, at age 17, Helen married Nikifor Blavatsky, a 51-year old government officer. The marriage lasted only a short time, but the experience must not have been very bad for Helen, for she kept the name of her ex-husband for the rest of her life. She married another man, but she never felt herself emotionally tied.

A constant traveller

Helen decided to devote herself to travel when she was 20. When she became famous, she said she had spent seven years in Tibet, where she had been instructed in the ancient culture of the Lamas and the Hindus. Every time she returned to Russia, her family observed that she was larger and more nervous. She reached a weight of 105 kg, though she was not very tall. This was no obstacle to the fascination she created in people for her wealth of ideas, her ability to explain them, and her sincerity.

In 1870, she decided to travel to the United States, where Ignatius L. Donnelly's ideas about Atlantis were gaining a large following. In New York, she met Henry Steele Olcott to organise the Theosophical Association. They composed the word together, from the Greek terms for 'god' and 'wisdom'. The association was dedicated to the study of ancient enigmas, such as those related to the pyramids and the origin of the universe and humanity.

Madame Blavatsky became the leader of an important spiritual movement, from which she gathered the experience to write *The Secret Doctrine*, a work in two volumes about the science of the occult, based on the mysterious *Book of Dzyan*, which only she seemed to know of. In this text, she claimed to have established contact with spirits from Atlantis and Lemuria, the continent that created a compendium of Eastern and Western philosophies.

The Lemurians formed part of the third of seven races that gave shape to mankind. The world in which they lived occupied the Southern Hemisphere (Africa, Asia, the Indian Ocean, and parts of the Pacific). They had hermaphroditic physiques and bore a 'third eye', which corresponded to their psychic energy. The fourth race corresponded to the people of Atlantis, where the inhabitants were descendants of the Lemurians, as the race had perished along with their continent, sunk below the sea millions of years before.

The seer and theosopher Helen Blavatsky was convinced that the survivors of Lemuria and Atlantis escaped to Asia and central Europe, where they became Hindu and Tibetan priests and the great Russian and German thinkers.

Through quartz crystals

W. Scott-Elliot is considered one of the authors who wrote the best texts about lost continents, such as Atlantis and Lemuria. Whether or not the tales are believable, nobody can question that his work *The Tale of the Lost Atlantis and Lemuria*, published in 1925, makes enjoyable reading, whilst also being of a literary quality that puts it at the top of its genre. The fact that he never presented any original ideas, apart from some that he claimed he had received via some 'quartz crystals' that enabled him to connect with the wisdom of the past, does not discredit him.

Scott-Elliot said the Atlanteans lived in a totalitarian society, governed by a type of aristocracy that had created a large number of technological marvels. For example, they possessed aerial vehicles in which they travelled around the continent at a speed of 100 mph. These devices were driven by a fuel called 'vril', which provided them with a driving force similar to that of modern aircraft. Furthermore, the continent of Atlantis covered five million years of history.

During this long period, the island suffered four cataclysms. The first took place 800,000 years ago, when the island continent took up almost the whole of the Atlantic Ocean. Some 200,000 years ago, part of the land disappeared, leaving two enormous islands: Ruta and Daitya. The third destruction took place 80,000 years ago and left nothing more above water than the island of Poseidonis, which was situated in the area that is now the Azores. The final destruction arrived in the year 9564 BC.

Scott-Elliot added to these dates that of the first emigration from Atlantis to Egypt 400,000 years ago, and he also tried to demonstrate that the Peruvian Incas existed 14,000 years ago.

With this contribution and the other three discussed in this chapter, we have given a representation of all the modern authors who have written about Atlantis. There are many whom we have not mentioned, simply due to limits of space. All that remains is to recommend the works of some of them, as the way they present their subjects can spark the imagination in new and unimaginable directions.

Chapter XIV

WAS PARADISE LOST?

The existence of a sixth continent

At this point, we may ask ourselves the question: What does modern science think about the enigma of Atlantis? As we hope to have shown, this question forms part of one of the great controversies of history. Most modern scientists believe that an Atlantic continent did exist, while others prefer to locate it in an area in the south-west of Spain.

The German investigator K. Bilau is one of those who support the idea that Plato neither invented his facts, nor used metaphor. He is convinced that thousands of years ago there was a great movement of the continents that transformed the previous oceans and seas. With the measurements made by the oceanographers as support, he uses the elevation of the Atlantic bed, especially in one strip that is equidistant from America and Africa, as a basis for his theories. For this reason, he mentions an 'Atlantic crossmember' between the western and eastern sides of an immense basin.

Bilau believes the complete disappearance of a sixth continent should not be considered an extraordinary event, as a rising or sinking of sea level by 9,842 feet, which is what happened, would not be a catastrophe for the planet:

We can imagine a terrestrial globe 42.6 feet in diameter. If we marked on this sphere the relative depth of the ocean in the equatorial region, we would have to trace a line 8.2 feet thick. But if the diameter of the globe were only 1 m, we would be able to represent the depth of the ocean with no more than a thin layer of varnish, like the globes offered to the public.

In fact, the slightest alteration in the rotation of our planet would be sufficient to create changes to our coastlines that on a human scale would be huge, but from a geo-mathematical point of view would be insignificant. From this perspective, Bilau unites his theories to those of Plato when he adds the following:

In the south-west region of Europe, sunk in the depths of the Atlantic, now lies Atlantis. No more than the tallest mountain peaks are now visible, as the Azores and the Canaries. All its sources of cold and hot water described by ancient authors still flow as they did thousands of years ago, and the lakes that decorated the mountains of the continent have been transformed into underwater lakes. If we believe Plato's accounts, to the south we will find the isle of Dollabarata, and there, on a high rise of land, in the exact centre of a wide and regular valley well protected from the winds, stood the splendid Poseidonis. But we have been deprived of the good fortune of being able to contemplate that active cultural centre of an unknown society of prehistoric origin, as we are separated from the city and its golden gates by 9,842.5 feet of water. It is incredible that scientists have searched everywhere for Atlantis, but have not paid heed to that little mark, which despite everything, was clearly described by Plato.

The opposing theories

The reverse side of Bilau's argument states that the American and African continents were part of one land mass in prehistoric times, until this land was split when the continents began to separate. In support of this point of view Alfred Wegener drew attention to the fact that the East Coast of America would fit perfectly into the West Coast of Africa.

174

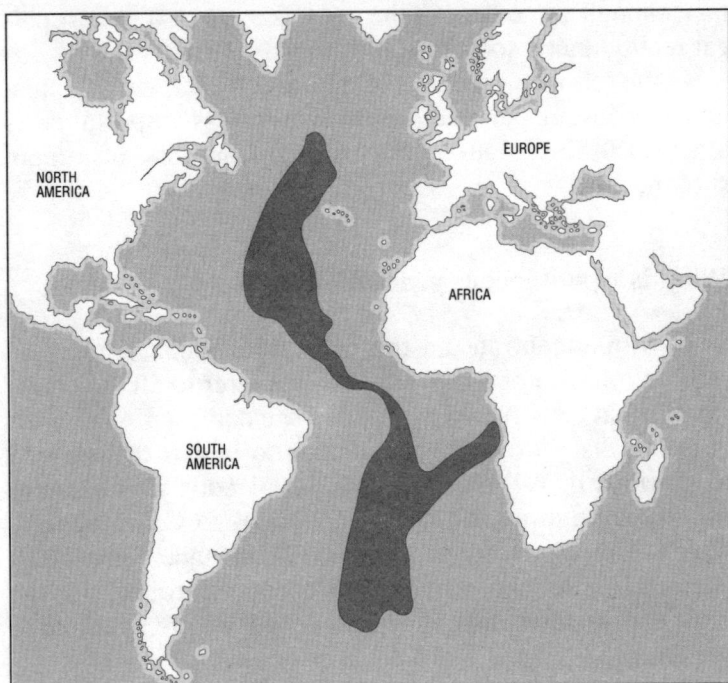

Figure 31. Thousands of years ago, there was a sixth continent between Africa, America, and Europe.

He also points out the many resemblances between the southern coast of South America, the coast of Australia, and the south-east coast of Africa, which suggest an original single land mass that was later to separate. In the same way as the edges of a torn sheet of paper fit together, so do the limits of dry land, with the only difference that minor changes have appeared in the coastline with the passing of time.

As we can see, a part of the investigations into Atlantis followed a different course. We are fully convinced that the ancient legend is based on real evidence and that the utopian tale of the island continent offered certain elements of truth.

Archaeologists have found a concordance between ancient historical information and the investigation work carried out until the present day. Few would make so bold as to affirm without a shadow of doubt that Atlantis is pure fantasy, though some believe the myth is more of a philosophical reality than a solid fact, fulfilling a spiritual need.

In the following sections of this last chapter, we will present a different perspective, in which less importance is attached to the location of Atlantis for the sake of a more sublime aim.

What is 'spontaneous generation'?

If we concentrate on the most traditional history, on reaching the era of the pyramids – we refer to all the civilisations that constructed pyramids – we come across a series of events that presents a contradiction so evident that we tend to overlook it. We can appreciate this paradox after examining human evolution from Neanderthal to Cro Magnum, which formed prehistory. Suddenly, we are taken on to civilisations like Jericho, Al-Ubaid, Mohengo-Daro, etc. Do the most conservative historians believe that we are too blind to see the gap?

After a close following of humankind's journey from walking apes to the discovery of fire, having made the first bone weapons, we see their continuing evolution. And when they started to sharpen arrowheads and the first flint knives, we are told that they were already constructing villages with canals carrying water from one side to another, that they controlled agriculture and built stables to shelter their livestock. But they mention nothing of perfect social organisations like the Egyptians or the Incas. And what can we say about the industrial organisation discovered in Harappa that Piggott told us about?

The Palaeolithic age required millions of years, but the following leap took place in…how much time? José Alvárez López calls this leap the 'theory of the spontaneous generation of cultures' and bases it on the ideas of the American school of archaeology, used to explain the surprising evolution of the Toltecs, the Incas, the Mayans, and other pre-Columbian civilisations.

It seems a total contradiction of ideas that we accept that the human race needed two million years to learn how to use a flint knife and then, suddenly, was miraculously able to organise societies superior to those of today, with more perfect languages (Sanskrit, Greek, Latin, Quechua, etc.), technology that has not been surpassed by some civilisations of the present day (the potter's wheels of the first Egyptian dynasty), and who produced an art of genius.

Logic forces us to accept that an exceptional event must have occurred. At a certain point, perhaps 11,600 years ago, some 'wise professors' arrived at many places on the Earth to instruct the most receptive peoples. They did this without frightening the races, for they knew themselves to be the bearers of knowledge that could drive ignorant beings mad. They mixed with the primitive tribes and began to extend ideas, in the simplest forms, which aroused curiosity as they developed and, above all, the necessity to obtain the utmost benefits from the new learnings.

All these wonders were achieved in a single millennium, and in the two millennia that followed, the state of humankind almost regressed as a result of continuous warfare and the pressure religious inquisitions. Only the Renaissance, and the consequent need to know more and more, fed the souls of the eighteenth century and accomplished a partial reparation of the damage. But this accomplishment only dates back two centuries.

With the aim of escaping this absurd history that archaeology has provided us, we have no choice but to take reality to a different sphere. One acceptable proposal would be to travel to the volcanic islands of the Atlantic. In the atolls that were found there during the glacial age, we are sure to find the best signs to follow the development of humankind over millions of years.

The Red Men

In a previous chapter, we wrote about the 'peaceful volcanoes' that provided the hot water that was used to create geothermic energy in Iceland and Greenland and converted them into paradisiacal lands. During the Glacial Age, the waters of the Atlantic must have been frozen, and only the existence of volcanoes could create an atollic micro-climate in which humans could survive.

Into this world the Red Men were born: their bodies exposed to the lukewarm sun, well-allied with the warm waters that sprang from the ground, being surrounded by permanent ice. They had no fear of this ice, however, as they were inhabiting what we could call an 'Enclosed Paradise'.

Many historians are convinced that the most cultured primitive humans were red-skinned. This is supported by the existence of names such as Adam, Cario, Phoinike, Pellops, Seth, Canaan, and many others. Each of these words is a synonym, in various languages, of 'red man' or even of 'red Atlantean'.

In his work *Reconstruction of Atlantis*, José Alvárez López tells us:

As an important boundary mark, we can say that the descendants of these Red Men lost the pigment in their skin, and archaeologists of today must turn to ingenious explanations to clarify why the Phoenicians were called red (Phoinike, in Greek, means 'red'), why the Cretans were called Kaftor, and why Adam means 'red'. Why do the paintings in the tomb of Tutenkhamon – and all the other Egyptians – paint people in a scarlet red – today unknown in our races – the colour of prawns. In the case of the Etruscans, an archaeologists explains with charming naivety: "They painted their bodies with minium". The last Red People were the North American 'Redskins', today intermixed and almost extinct. In our day, some people who live on frozen beaches or go in for snow sports develop a primitive red tinge. The conditions for this development are well-known: frozen water and strong sun, circumstances that today give status to the summer holiday-makers of certain famous health resorts. Strangely enough, these are the conditions that must have prevailed in the atolls of the Glacial Atlantic.

The need for Pyramids

Many great ancient civilisations are connected with the pyramids. Their construction was no whim, but had a significant scientific base. If we analyse the pyramid from a practical point of view, we can see that their form provides a stable base, as the whole weight of the building is at the base. The ancient peoples built their constructions to last a long time, as well as to stand up to hurricanes, typhoons, earthquakes, and other atmospheric and geological phenomena.

The problem posed by the pyramidal form is only revealed when we consider it as a residence, as it is very difficult to construct a way to ascend to higher levels. The red-skinned people of Colorado resolved this problem a long time before

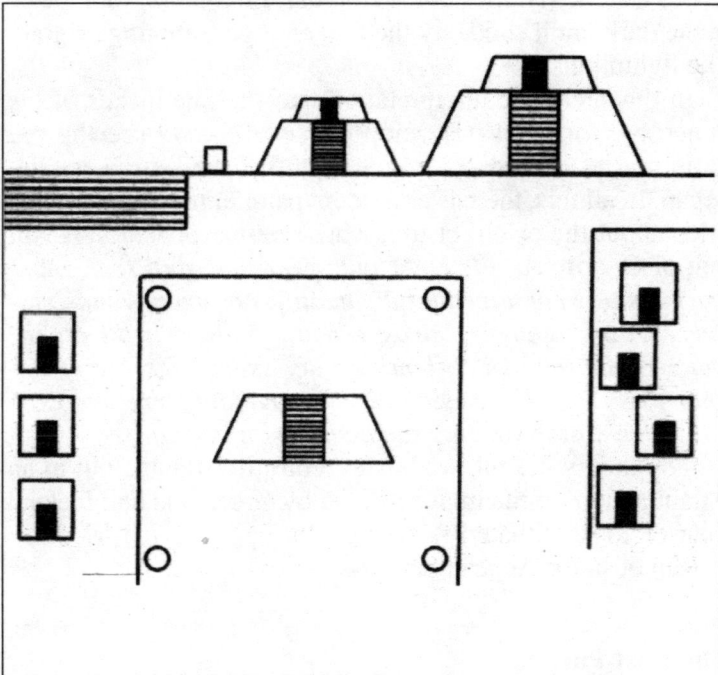

Figure 32. The Mexican city of Teotihuacan, where the pyramids formed the centre of all activity.

the Spanish conquerors arrived, with 'monoblocks', pathways that ingeniously encircled the pyramid building.

As it does not bother us to talk of 'supernatural' elements, we may observe the use of 'space doors' on the pyramids where spaceships from distant planets landed, or the aircraft mentioned by Cayce and Scott-Elliot. The pioneers of science fiction films and comics made great use of these pyramidal buildings to represent landscapes on Mars or other planets in our solar system.

A new perspective that we cannot ignore is that volcanoes have the form of truncated pyramids. In the most remote theology that we know, that of 'Hermopolis', the Sun is said to have had its origin on Earth, where it was born on the Primordial Red Mountain from an egg laid by the Earth. Pirenne explains that the 'red mountain' (Tehennu) sprouted from the 'basic waters' (Nun), but the first part of creation took place in the dark, until suddenly the Sun emerged, shining brightly like lightning.

In this alchemic interpretation that Pirenne makes of the 'Theology of Thot' (Hermopolis), we should see the red mountain as a volcano, which signifies the sea where life began. In all this, there is an evident parallel with modern theories about the origin of life, whose best explanation is still that of Oparin: *All life came out of a primordial sea, whose warm waters contained large quantities of amino acids produced by the lightning, the oxygen and nitrogen in the air, the water of the sea and carbon dioxide. As the presence of sulphur was crucial, the essential red mountain came into existence, the atollic volcano surrounding an interior sea.*

The theory has allowed us to return to Atlantis, but to an Atlantis more of the image offered by Greenland and Iceland than of those situated further south, opposite the Mediterranean or in the Aegean Sea.

The Lost Paradise

The great importance that the Ancients gave to the binomial Earth-Sun continues to be an almost totally unanswered question. If we consider that the necessary energies come from two sources, the Earth and the Sun, it is easier to comprehend the reason why the mythical gods were named with two words: Atum-Aton, Amon-Ra, Osiris-Isis, Iahve-Shamash, New Jerusalem-Cordero, etc.

However, what we are looking at here is the Sun-Volcano relation, as it constitutes the synthesis of many religions. We also can observe the essence of the Great Pyramid. In the old traditions of the ancient peoples, it is said that the happiness of humankind was only obtained after the marriage of the Earth and the Sun. But this is represented by a volcano, the masculine component that was always joined with the feminine: the Earth or the New Jerusalem.

There is nothing more suitable to represent the 'happy couple' than the sphere, which encloses the City of Peace – Atlantis. The combination of reality is completed, which leads us to recall that in a sea of the Glacial Age, the only possibility of survival was provided by the convenient volcanic atolls of the Atlantic. From these were born and evolved hundreds of thousands of human beings and their paradisiacal world. Culture came later, when they understood that they did not need to work, though they continued to do so.

Aristotle gives the best explanation: *inspired human creativity is born into freedom, without the pressure of urgent need.* These peoples were able to enjoy poetry, legends, and a religion that was pleasant both for the gods and for their worshippers. They created art and play; they evolved in love and learned to control their sexuality. And one day, they created mathematics and philosophy.

These red-skinned people, naked or adorned with flowers, worked with gold to shape decorations for their temples or their festivals, which were continuous. In general, they obtained the precious metal without having to extract it from mines; they simply gathered it from the generous surface that they found close by.

Have we not just described Paradise on Earth? It sprang up like water, as a simple deduction. But these beings who lost their Eden when Atlantis sank were very different from our human race of today. Their existence was so easy because they knew how not to exceed an ideal population, which leads us to the idea that sex was regarded as sublime, almost as a rite that could lose its benefits if abused.

They must have been a race of pacifists, proof of which is given by the fact that the first wars and pillaging do not appear in history until the year 2006 BC, at the exact moment when the hordes of bushmen, whose origin is unknown, appeared and destroyed Ur. From these times came Abraham, as the Bible tells, and from the same setting emerged the events of the world, which were the beginnings of all the negative aspects that we have inherited.

Was there an Earthly Paradise on Atlantis? If it was so, we could identify it with the Atlantis of Plato's work, Homer's Scheria, and the Eden described in the Bible. As we know, the word 'eden' means 'closed garden' in Aramaic, just as the term 'paradaisos', from which 'paradise' comes, means 'hunting ground', or in ancient Persian, an enclosed place.

In this way, we find ourselves once again at the atolls of the Atlantic, which we talked about in previous chapters. We find this reference in the Bible when, after the expulsion of Adam and Eve, it is written: *they went to live to the east of Paradise*. According to this, the Atlantic is the birth place of humanity.

Mankind was expelled from Paradise 12,000 years ago, and we have never been able to return. The expectations of the future are far from the Atlantic atolls, whose memory survived with the red-skinned people. Today, the Earth is a 'spherical atoll', alongside a volcano perhaps even greater than all earlier ones: Atomic Energy.

At this point, we pose the question that José Alvárez López asked: *Will the human race ever live again in a Spherical Atlantis – in a new City of Peace – or will their world be blown into thousands of pieces by a New Volcano?*

The enigmas live on

We do not want to finish on a pessimistic note, though the threat of the 'New Volcano' may not be forgotten while nuclear power stations exist that will have to be buried when the time comes, as required international law, and which will then leave a lethal legacy in the form of the radioactivity that will remain for another 12,000 years. Unless, of course, somebody invents a cleaner way of creating power, which we are convinced will happen.

Atlantis was a paradise that gave birth to the Great Masters who created the civilisations of the pyramids and, most importantly, paved the way for humanity to make the most important qualitative step in history and accomplish in one millennium more than everything we know today. We can also confirm that it was located in the Atlantic.

Plato was right, of this we are certain. Moreover we accept the idea that Tartessus represents, more than any other theory, the true Atlantis. However, we believe that a different interpretation existed about the origin of the myth. We find it difficult to accept that, in prehistoric times, while in five continents of the world human beings were still almost primates without even the knowledge of fire, there was a sixth where people flew in aircraft, used 'stones of fire' to communicate with the spirits, and above all, lived in paradise.

Out of pure intuition we have to consider the possibility of extraterrestrial beings, gods from distant planets who set up in Atlantis a kind of academy for scholars, who they allowed to live in paradise while they taught them their vast knowledge. Later on, as they were dealing with beings of an imperfect nature, even though it was only in a tiny number of their chromosomes, ambition and neglect for spirituality took over, which finally led to the Great Cataclysm.

But this was neither climatic nor geological, but something internal, as though all the power accumulated in the island-continent had exploded. In this way the Atlanteans were scattered in all directions of the wind, and the sixth island continent was sunk beneath the ocean.

This is our version, which does not clarify many enigmas, for it is now left for the readers to choose their own preferences from the offered options. We have laid out, often almost synoptically, the various paths that lead to Atlantis, and we admit that there are still more, which for questions of space we have not been able to offer. However, we have mentioned all the main theories. The subject is open to new investigation, which this book invites.

In the same way that the city of Troy was finally discovered, and that other cities have been uncovered which nobody believed existed, some day we will be able to finally blow away the mists that surround the myth of Atlantis. We live in overly materialistic times, but in each and every one of us, a large part is open to wonders and marvels. We do not lose the hope that the 'unbelievable will come true' – we only hope that it happens soon.

BIBLIOGRAPHY

Álvarez López, José: *Reconstruction of Atlantis*
Álvarez López, José: *Reality of Atlantis*
Atienza, Juan G: *Survivors of Atlantis*
Bergier, Jacques and Pauwels, Louis: *The Morning of the Magicians*
Bergier, Jacques and Pauwels, Louis: *The Rebellion of the Magicians*
Berlitz, Charles: *Atlantis: The eighth continent*
Carnac, Pierre: *History begins in Bimini*
Cayce, Edgar Evans: *Mysteries of Atlantis*
Deruelle, Jean: *The Challenge of the Atlanteans: The prehistoric revolution*
Guirao, P: *The Enigma of the Maps of Piri Reis*
Guirao, P: *The Enigma of Tiahuanaco*
Huttin, Serge: *Unknown Civilisations*
Kolosimo, Peter: *Civilisations of Silence*
Luce, J. V: *The End of Atlantis*
Lleget, Marius: *Atlantis*
Saurat, Denis: *Atlantis*
Sánchez Dragó, Fernando: *Gargoris and Habidis. A magic history of Spain* (4 volumes)
Tomas, Andrew: *The Secrets of Atlantis*
Tomas, Andrew: *We are not the first*
Zalabarda García Muro, José Luis: *Atlantis*
Number 1 of the magazine "Enigmas"

INDEX